The Bobby Dazzlers

by the same author

BILTON

The Bobby Dazzlers

ANDREW MARTIN

faber and faber

First published in Great Britain in 2001
by Faber and Faber Limited
3 Queen Square London WC1N 3AU
Published in the United States by Faber and Faber, Inc.,
an affiliate of Farrar, Straus and Giroux, New York

Typeset by Faber and Faber
Printed in England by Clays plc, St Ives

A CIP record for this book
is available from the British Library

ISBN 0–571–20103–2

10 9 8 7 6 5 4 3 2 1

Prologue

'You're on the spot, you know,' said Cooper.

'What's that?' I said.

I'd heard him but not *properly* because we were playing squash. Greengrass is the only YOI in the country to have a squash court. I don't know how it came to *have* a squash court – I think they must've built it by accident or something, or just got carried away and built a really big cell. It was basically for screws but you could have a session during Saturday afternoon association if you were red band and put your name down. Next door was the gym, and through the wall came the sound of thirty nonces doing squat thrusts in time to the bawling of a screw, but even though they were only nonces they were making the whole place shudder.

'What did you say?' I said to Cooper.

'Five one,' said Cooper, getting ready to serve.

So I hadn't heard him, and now he hadn't heard me.

Cooper was nineteen, same age as I was, and we were both in the YOI part of Greengrass (the other part was a Category 'C' nick with a big sexual offenders unit). He was in for twocking – taking cars without consent, like about a hundred and fifty of them. Cooper was a twocking machine, and nearly blind with it. He kept his specs on for squash, and kept prodding them back up his nose with the middle finger of his right hand. He was very good at squash though, so he'd take a point off me, then shove his specs back up his nose with this middle finger of his and, after a while, it got to be a very annoying combination.

It was a good job that Cooper wore specs because otherwise he wouldn't have had a face: his head was just a kind of blank tube. I'd got to know him when he'd sold me a slim jim and twenty janglers, which might or might not unlock some Volvo 240s, in exchange for an eighth of black, a deal that said a lot about Cooper's opinion of the Volvo 240. He didn't even want one passing through his hands.

'You've been put on the spot,' said Cooper again, when the score was six one, and I was lying on my back, wiped out after quite a good rally that Cooper had won.

'What are you waffling on about?' I said, getting up.

'There's a guy out to do you harm.'

'In here?'

'Outside.'

'What's his name?'

'Neville.'

Cooper served up.

It was a beautiful serve, and I couldn't fish it out of the corner.

'Neville?' I said. 'What kind of fucking name is that?'

'It's *his* name.'

I didn't know any Neville.

'He's been put on to you by some other guy,' said Cooper. 'It's the other guy that wants you fucked up.'

'Fucked up in what way?'

'Big time,' said Cooper, and served.

I was losing heart for the game now. A lot of things were coming into my head that I didn't want there. Cooper served up again, and I ignored the ball.

'Stop firing fucking squash balls at me, and tell me what's going on.'

Cooper looked at me with the usual expression on his face: nothing.

'Why does anybody want me dead?' I said, sounding like a wuss.

'Well, this guy who's been in touch with Neville, and who's actually a mate of Neville's . . . he says you killed his kid.'

I felt like sitting down, because I was spinning back in time five years, back to when I was fifteen, long before I'd started doing houses. I could only repeat what Cooper had said.

'He wants me dead because he says I've killed his kid?'

'Sounds like a good reason to me,' said Cooper, who was hitting the ball for himself now, going faster and faster, big black plimoes squeaking.

'You're taking the piss,' I said.

Cooper didn't say anything to that and, after a while, these were the words that came out of my mouth: 'It was an accident.'

'Yeah?' said Cooper, still hitting.

'It was five years ago,' I said.

'But the kid's still dead, isn't he?' said Cooper. 'That's the trouble.'

On the other side of the wall the nonces had started playing volleyball, shouting their nonsense shouts.

'Who is this Neville?' I said.

'G,' said Cooper, battering the ball.

'Don't give me that fucking rubbish,' I said. '. . . Where does he live?'

'London.'

'Can't you be more specific?'

'East.'

'And is this Neville some kind of nonsense case?'

Cooper shook his head and sat down so that I could see his horrible straggly todger swinging inside his shorts.

'He's a very cool guy, and he's got, like, principles. He's the sort of bloke . . . if he's paid to do something, especially by a mate, he does it unless . . .'

'Unless what?'

Cooper was cleaning his specs on his raggedy old vest. As he did this his eyeballs were going crazy, slithering about in their holes. It was nearly enough to make you feel sorry for the bloke.

'Unless someone else pays him more not to,' he said, putting the glasses back on, and instantly looking normal again.

'So if I pay him, he won't top me, is that what you're saying?'

'It's a possibility. But I'll have to have a word.'

'How do you know about all this?'

'Brother.'

'*Who's* fucking brother?' I said.

The trouble with Cooper was he didn't use enough words when he talked.

'Mine.'

'He knows Neville?'

'They get wasted together sometimes.'

Something had come back into my life that I thought had gone. I was all emptied out, and Cooper could see that, but he wasn't reacting in any way at all. I'd known the score straightaway; the paymaster was Cameron Lacey's old man – a person I'd written off, because he was divorced from Lacey's old lady and hadn't been seen in York for years. Evidently he was on a vigilante mission.

All the next week I was on the fraggle, not talking in associations, not sleeping at nights, and taking a lot of abuse as a result. I spent all my time thinking about Cameron Lacey, and what had happened, and thinking about Neville. I could picture him in my mind's eye: a big guy.

Exactly one week later I was on project in the playing field of a deserted infants school with Cooper. All around us was the countryside of Lincolnshire – hazy fields with broken cars and caravans in them, not a very inspiring sight. Summer was coming to the north Midlands, but very slowly. We were supposed to be installing drainage, or something; the fact is, I didn't know what the bloody hell we were supposed to be doing because I only had one thing in mind. I walked up to Cooper who was standing in front of a bonfire that he'd decided to waste time by making. Above it, the air wobbled. He was supposed to be burning branches, but actually he was just staring into the fire, probably with a head full of cars. Every so often he'd prod his glasses back up his nose with the middle finger of his right hand, only this time he was wearing big orange gloves, like all of us working in that field.

'You're in the clear,' he said.

'Good,' I said.

'As long as you can get twenty grand to Neville.'

I took off my gloves, which had sweat sloshing in the finger ends, and looked at my hands. They were small in comparison with Neville's – probably.

'I'm fucked then, aren't I?'

'Ten grand is what Neville's getting off the other guy so he's, like, doubled it.'

'That's nice of him.'

I threw a stick on the fire for Cooper, but he didn't seem to even notice.

'What if I paid him *eleven* grand?' I asked him.

'No, because the other guy's Neville's mate, and you killed the kid you see, so the other guy's got right on his side, and Neville always likes to do what's right. Depending on the money.'

'Well he can't get me if I'm in here, can he?'

As I said this we were actually standing in a field as I've already mentioned, but Cooper knew what I meant.

'That's right,' he said. 'But you're out next week, aren't you? If you can get the cash together, here's where you've got to take it. I'd say you've got about a month.'

He took his gloves off, and put his hand in his overalls, coming out with the sort of little piece of paper you saw every day in Greengrass: 'Greengrass HMP & YOI', it said. 'The future is what counts.' Underneath, you could write notes, and Cooper had written a London phone number.

'That's a filling station near Greenwich, right? It's our kid's. He'll pass the money on to Neville.'

'How do I know your brother's not just a chancer who's worked out this little set-up for his own benefit?'

'Well,' said Cooper, taking his glasses off and making his eyeballs go weird again, 'you know it's not a set-up because you know it's all true. You did kill the kid, whose name was Cameron Lacey, and the kid's dad is pissed off. He's dodgy, so I've heard, and this is his way of dealing with it: get Neville on the case. I didn't have to tell you any of this, it's a waste of my fucking . . . breath, which I need to *live*, so don't start disrespecting my fucking brother, you little fucking northern twat.'

I didn't talk to Cooper again after that.

Part One *Bryan Butteridge and*
Cameron Lacey

One

Saturday evening in York; summertime; pubs doing good business, emergency services standing by.

The tourists have gone . . . wherever they go, and I'm rattling down Micklegate on my knackered Palm Beach, going to see Bill. I used to be a serious BMXer, but I'd come down in the world, bike-wise. The problem with the Palm Beach was the mudguard, which was scraping against the front tyre, so I was leaning across the handlebars and holding it up – which was a degrading thing for somebody who'd just turned twenty to be doing.

I recognized some of the lads going along Micklegate, and the ones who recognized *me* had a particular expression on their faces: respect. Not because of my look, which was far from cutting edge (Nike Air Max trainers, cheap combat, boring blue T) or because I was hard, but because I'd just got out of YOI. As a matter of fact I was still on licence at this time, and there was at least a month to go until my SED. I'd heard nothing from so-called Neville, and heard nothing *about* him, so I was beginning to think the whole thing was a wind-up.

It was nine o'clock, and the evening was changing from light blue to dark as I turned into Rougier Street, foot scraping on the ground speedway style, and somebody on the pavement shouted out: 'Lights!'

'Fuck off, you fat bastard!' I yelled back, although actually I had no idea whether the person who'd shouted had been fat or not.

Two minutes later I was rattling past the 'no cycling' signs of the Museum Gardens, with more sweat coming out of my body than could possibly have been *in* my body, then through the high black gates, heading east, parallel with the Scarborough railway line. The night was filled with the smell of flowers and smoke as a dusty train rattled past on the Scarborough line, sounding just like a lot of metal being dragged over another lot of metal – too loud. I don't like trains, even little ones, so I sort of held my breath as it went by.

Eventually I came to Bill's terraced house, which was opposite a church. I locked the Palm Beach against the church railings, walked over the road and knocked on his door. Bill's neighbour nodded at me whilst I waited. The bloke had a hell of a lot of grey hair, and a hearing-aid. He was sitting on his doorstep cleaning shoes, and he'd put a newspaper down to catch any specks of polish, protecting the ancient city of York, you see, even though there was only the footpath underneath. From inside his house – with that echo that tells you the radio's in the kitchen – came the sound of that nonsense case, Bryan Butteridge, who actually had two voices: a normal one, and the 'on' voice, which is what I was hearing at that moment, and which needs to be written down like this:

'Wherever I go around t' world,' Butteridge was saying, *'whether it be Leeds, 'uddersfield, Bradford or Wakefield, people allus want to know one thing: what's 'appenin' to Yorkshire puddin's?'*

A very likely story, I thought, as Bill opened the door.

Bill was a criminal mastermind in inverted commas, and the only guy I really respected or trusted. If ever so-called Neville came looking for me, I'd turn to Bill for help.

He was a scrawny bloke with hypnotizing green eyes, and he looked like a Yorkshireman should: he had what's called *tone*. He could handle all situations, and was a very bright guy

– he must've been because he'd been iffy for years, but had no form. He had a part share in a mail-order business that sold CDs, and he did insurance for rock bands or something, but he was also a fence and dealt dope. Through his legitimate businesses, he could absorb a lot of cash; launder it. He was small time I suppose, but I think he liked it that way because he had outside interests: Bill was into his family.

Bill was at least ten years older than me, and the first thing he said to me was that he'd kill me if I grassed him up, but that was only to be expected. Over the next three years I nicked VCRs etc. for him, and we started getting on quite well, but he always treated me like a kid, and I could never have called myself a mate of Bill's, which was fine by me. A lot of people have got a lot of friends. Personally I think it's all bullshit.

'All right?' said Bill, opening his door and jamming a mobile phone into the waistband of his Levis. (Being an older man, Bill always preferred fitted trousers. I used to think that he had this old skool Rolling Stones tip going, dating from the time when that lot still had some bollocks.)

I waited for Bill to say come in, then I stepped quite cautiously into his rowdy little house, which had a good atmosphere, giving you the idea that a party could start any minute just by spontaneous combustion. Behind him the living-room door was open, and there were three women, sprawling with their great long legs everywhere. One was Bill's wife, Ingrid, who was not naturally blond, but *was* naturally beautiful. She half nodded at me, giving me a look that could've meant anything, and making me self-conscious about my complexion, which is not the best. Back then, I was still suffering from these swellings on the face that came and went very slowly. I called them brambles.

'I want you to meet a friend of mine,' said Bill, closing the

living-room door. 'He's up from London for the day. I mean
. . . he's OK, but he's a bit . . .'

'What?' I said, after a while.

Bill produced a lighter with the speed of a gunslinger, then
slowly lit a Silk Cut.

'He's got one of those . . .'

Bill dragged on the fag, with a faraway look in his eyes.

'It's just that when he starts his . . .'

This was all becoming quite disturbing.

'Anyway,' said Bill, snapping out of it, 'you'll see for yourself in a minute.'

I nodded.

'That's fine, Bill,' I said, 'but is it all right to talk in front of
him?'

Going upstairs, Bill quickly put my mind at ease.

'The guy's got a string of convictions as long as his arm.
You can say whatever you fucking well want.'

'What's his thing?' I asked, following Bill up the stairs.

'Houses,' said Bill.

That was my thing too.

'How was Wealstun?' said Bill.

(What the hell is this?)

'I wasn't in Wealstun,' I said. 'I'm too young. I was in
Greengrass.'

'Oh,' he said.

I was quite pissed off that Bill didn't want to hear about
Greengrass.

'What's this mate of yours called?' I asked.

'Dean Martin,' said Bill, as we moved from the top of his
staircase to a ladder which lead up to his attic.

'Not *the* Dean Martin, I assume?'

'What you say?' said Bill, over the clattering of our feet on
the rungs.

12

'I said, "Not *the* Dean Martin?"'

The joke was wearing a bit thin by now.

'Oh yeah,' said Bill, moving on. 'Walter's here too.'

I didn't say anything to that.

There was a major bike-theft problem in York, and Walter Bowler was it. He smashed the locks with a hammer, after spraying on a plumber's freezing agent to make them more brittle. Bowler might do this at four o'clock in the afternoon in the middle of Coney Street or anywhere else in the middle of town. It was a kind of double bluff in that anyone passing by would automatically assume that anyone so obviously nicking a bike could not actually be nicking a bike.

But they were wrong.

Age-wise, Bowler was between me and Bill – probably twenty-five. He reminded me of a stub or a stump or a bollard. His big face had a bulging, desperado look, which I reckon was because he was ugly, and *knew* he was ugly, but couldn't accept it. He didn't have much hair, and what there was of it came straggling outwards from his big round face in a way that reminded me of a kid's drawing of the sun. He usually wore jogging pants, Cat boots and a Ben Sherman shirt.

Walter Bowler always seemed to have a lot of mud on these casual clothes, and he lived with his evil dad on a smallholding cum scrap heap just outside York that was full of hay bales bursting out of bin bags, burnt-out ice-cream vans, and broken old cranes and suchlike that were full of scabby hens and rats and other creatures with diseases.

I didn't like Walter Bowler, and he didn't like me. It looks weird written down but I think he was jealous of me. I suppose he thought I was a smartarse, and was worried that Bill rated me higher than him. I didn't like him because I was pretty sure he'd grassed me up, leading to my first burglary charges, so with Bowler I was always looking for the sideswipe, trouble coming out of the blue, and I used to think that Bill should've been on the look out for those things too. I couldn't understand why he stuck with him.

When I put my brambly head through the loft hatch, the first thing I saw was Bowler standing in the corner next to the skylight, looking through it, holding a bottle of barley wine. He got pissed very slowly, but on his favourite tipple of booze and toot he was liable go off like a rocket.

'It's public enemy number one,' said Bowler, when he saw me.

Next to him was some sort of cockney pinhead sitting on a sofa. He was stroking Bill's Mike Tyson-lookalike dog, and talking to Bill's pretty daughter who was eleven or so, and bright with it. The cockney nodded at me as I looked at him. I could smell spliff, Indian food and barley wine. I was staring at the cockney in amazement, trying to figure out who the hell he was, when Bowler started insulting me again.

'I'd like to know why you've bothered locking that bike up,' he said.

'You should know better than anyone,' I said.

'Take that thing off-roading through Knavesmire Woods . . . it'd fucking fall apart.'

'But I don't want to ride it off-road,' I said. 'I want to ride it *on* the road, if you can get your head around that.'

Bowler started eyeballing me, with his big basketball head throbbing.

'So vat's like . . . ver cockney classics and fings,' the cockney was saying to the girl.

He had that Londoner's speech impediment: couldn't say '*th*'.

'You mean like "Knees Up Mother Brown" or something?' said Bill's girl.

'Nah. Ver cockney classics you see . . . it's like . . .' He

14

started making a sort of grinding, gurgling noise, then he stopped and said: 'Name vat tune. "Ver Drugs Don't Work" by Ver Verve. And check vis.' The noise started again. Grinding and gurgling – even worse than before.

'Could you stop that please?' said Walter Bowler.

Bill gave Bowler a heavy look, and the cockney stopped. But he went on talking.

'Ver cockney classics,' he said, 'ver's hundreds . . . "Under My Fumb", Stones; "By Ver Time I Get To Phoenix", Glen Campbell; "If I Could Turn Back Time", Cher.'

I took in the cockney's appearance. He was thin but with quite broad shoulders, but then again a tiny little head. His trainers were the same as mine, Nike Air Max, which made me think: I've just *got* to get my hands on some Pumas. He was also wearing dodgy phat pants and not one but two Arsenal shirts – one on top of the other – which was odd because Dean actually supported West Ham, as I was to find out later.

The cockney stood up. There were bent foil cartons on the coffee table in front of him, and yellow sauce around his mouth. He wiped this with the back of his right hand, which was fair enough, but then he held that hand out to me.

There was a tattoo of a black bloke's head at the bottom of his thumb.

'Vis is ver guy?' he said to Bill as he shook my hand.

'It is,' said Bill, looking dead embarrassed, and passing me a spliff.

As Bill put a CD on, I took a hit on the joint and passed it to Dean.

'Nice one,' he said, ' . . . aw, nice tune!'

In fact, it was nothing of the sort. It was Metallica, or something. Bill was cool but he liked heavy metal . . . so maybe he *wasn't* all that cool actually. He'd once had a job as a DJ on hospital radio, and he'd been fired for playing 'Don't Fear The Reaper' by Blue Oyster Cult once too often. He didn't mean anything sinister by it, he just happened to like that particular tune.

'Would you say that was one of the cockney classics?' Bill's girl asked Dean when the racket had finished.

'Vat one?' said Dean, and he thought about it for a while. 'Not as such,' he said, then he turned to Bill. 'So we're going to screw vis TV guy, right?'

Bill looked across at me, moving his lighter between his twitchy fingers.

'What are you doing now?' he said.

'Now?' I said, getting an instant buzz from the way Bill was looking at me. 'What do you mean?'

'Are you free tonight to do something?'

'We'll screw vat TV guy, right?' said Dean again. 'Be fucking wicked.'

'Hang on,' I said. 'Are we talking about Bryan Butteridge?'

Bill nodded; his daughter was climbing down the ladder, making herself scarce right on cue.

'The two of you could do him,' said Bill. 'He bought a couple of paintings last week, they're worth a few grand.'

Bill often knew about big purchases made within the city.

'Paintings of what?'

'One's of a horse,' said Bill. 'The other one's a picture of Little Bo Peep, or somebody like that.'

I was looking at Bill in amazement.

'It's a fucking girl on a hill,' he said. 'You won't be able to miss it.'

'Is Butteridge on holiday?' I asked.

'Nope,' said Bill.

So he was asking me to do a job that was aggravated, risking a five-year term.

16

'I'm up for it,' said Dean, who'd started jumping about in the middle of the room. 'Be fucking sweet, y'know what I'm saying?'

Things were going too fast so, to buy time, I asked Bill: 'Do you want me to get Butteridge's video recorder as well?'

This seemed to make Bill pissed off.

'No, I fucking well don't want you to get his fucking video recorder. All right?'

I was somewhat confused. It wasn't as if Bill didn't have a lock-up garage in Askham Bryan with fifty VCRs in it. They were all he'd had off me in the past, apart from the odd set of car keys and some hi-fi bits. Maybe he was trying to move upscale or impress Dean Martin. But *why?*

I needed money, and I might be in need of twenty grand one day, but I didn't want anything to do with the cockney – I worked alone – and even though I didn't like to disappoint Bill I didn't owe him any favours.

'I'm just out of Greengrass,' I said, 'so every cozzer in York's going to have a picture of me in his back pocket.'

'Don't fucking flatter yourself,' said Bowler.

Dean had stopped jumping. Bill walked over to the hi-fi, and the CD was ejected, like a robot putting its tongue out in my direction.

'It's not that I don't want to do it,' I said. 'I do; but I'm still on licence, I've got a probation officer breathing down my fucking neck.'

Bill loaded up another CD, and stood there for a while with his back to me, fiddling with technology.

'Paintings from a York house,' he said, turning around, 'it's not your usual MO.'

'I know it's not, Bill,' I said, 'but . . .'

Bill moved his lips, chewing on nothing, which was his way of showing you he was pissed off.

'He's bottled out,' said Bowler.

Sometimes Bill would tell Bowler, on my behalf, to shut his fucking face, but not now.

'See yourself out,' said Bill, turning his back on me.

I had no choice but to go, so I started clumping down the ladder, red in the face, brambles all lit up. I walked across the street to the bike, thinking about what I would do next: go home and try to find a place in the house where Wilkinson, who was my legal guardian, was *not*. I stopped in the street, hearing the sound of a goods train. It's a noise that bothers me, because sooner or later, in amongst all the rattling, you'll get that little bacon slicer sound singing out. Then the train sound was obliterated by a police car racing across the junction at the bottom of Bill's road, which is another noise that bothers me. I hated police cars, which was obviously symbolic of something else, because police cars would be perfectly all right if it wasn't for police*men*. I was also thinking . . . paintings from a York house. It *wasn't* my usual MO. I'd always done things outside the city in the past, and I just could not afford to let Bill down. He was my financial lifeline, Bill was my whole future.

I turned around, walked back and knocked on his door.

'Now then,' Bill said, when he eventually opened up. I told him I'd do the job, and he said, 'Meet Dean in Exhibition Square at – what do you reckon – two thirty?'

'Sounds fine,' I said, thinking how weird it was that, even on business directly concerning Dean Martin, Dean Martin himself did not need to be asked his opinion. Bill looked at me as if to say: you can go now. But I didn't want to go.

'Dean seems a nice bloke,' I said, just to see what Bill would say.

'He's a fucking halfwit,' said Bill, who was very gently sort of back-heeling his baby, which was trying to climb over the

18

doorstep, 'but he'll do what you say.'

'Why's he staying with you?'

Bill seemed to be considering whether to give the answer to a question like that to the likes of me; then he picked the baby up and leant against his door frame.

'I was in London on a bit of business, and somebody introduced me to him. We had a chat, and I said, if you're ever in York, look me up.'

Bill nodded at his neighbour who was sitting there with his polish and his shoes, still at it.

'That was fucking yesterday,' Bill went on, a bit more quietly, 'and this morning he was knocking on my front door. I wouldn't mind, but he'd been boasting about how he'd never been north of bloody Kentish Town – that was the only reason I invited him here. I'd never have asked him to come to see me if I'd thought there was any chance of him coming to *see* me.'

'But why didn't you tell him to bugger off?'

'Let's just say that I'm obliged to be hospitable.'

'Because you've got some deals going through in London, right, Bill?'

Bill smiled at me – *very* patronizing – and left it at that.

'You all right for cash?' he said, as I was walking away.

'I've got ten quid left out of my discharge money,' I said.

Bill put his baby down on the doorstep, where it slowly toppled over, and gave me another twenty; then, making sure that the shoe-cleaning guy wasn't looking, he gave me a nice little lump of hash.

'Call me on the mobile tomorrow,' Bill said, 'and don't get fucking nicked.'

As I walked over the road to my bike, a bottle of barley wine fell behind me. I didn't bother looking up at the skylight.

Two

I never met my dad but, for a long time, I thought he actually *was* the dark-haired one out of a seventies cowboy series that I used to see repeated on a Sunday morning: *Alias Smith and Jones*. But then, as I got to be a bit more mature – six or seven – I thought, no, he can't actually *be* that one, he must just look like him, and whenever I think of my dad now that's the image I have in my head.

I can't remember exactly how I began to think that, but I know it was my mother's doing in some way. My mother's name was Christine, and that's what I called her. I think of her as being all in white: white face, white hair in a nice thick bob, white fluffy jumpers, white shoes – an angel who worked for British Rail and then, but not for long, for Great North Eastern Railways.

She was a personal assistant to a man who fancied her; she liked 'American Pie' by Don Maclean, and an early eighties disco song called 'Inside Out' by Odyssey. She liked football and had Sky TV; she didn't like Princess Di; she was a good swimmer.

Because she worked on the railways, Christine had free train travel, and she used to take me down to London. For this reason, I always thought that she was more than just a Yorkie. She had wings, somehow. At some stage on any trip down south we'd be sitting on the edge of the fountains in Trafalgar Square, eating ice-creams from a van with flags flying on the top of it. There always seemed to be one duck in the fountain, and Christine used to pretend it was the same one we saw every time.

Christine drove a Volkswagen Polo that she called Barbara, and she liked going out. When she *did* go out, a young woman called Gillian Myers would babysit. I fancied Gillian Myers even more than I fancied my mother, which made me feel extremely guilty. Despite Gillian usually being indoors (babysitting me) when Christine was out, she was Christine's best friend, and they would talk about her blokes. There was one who rode a motorbike; and another worked in the same office as Christine. I liked that – it seemed neat somehow. One of the blokes was written up in the paper for being drunk and disorderly on Lendal Bridge, which Christine thought was hilarious, but it didn't stop her going out with him – something else did, later. On a couple of occasions Christine started asking me how close she should let the blokes get to her on the sofa, and I didn't like that. I refused to express any opinion.

In 1992, when I was ten years old, Christine had her hair permed, and as soon as I saw her new look I started to blub; I could see that she was getting old, and that she was trying to do something about it. Nothing settled down after that bubble cut and, two days later, she was involved in a pile-up on the A64.

Lying in bed, with Gillian babysitting down below, I heard my uncle's voice. (I called him Uncle Alan then; I call him Wilkinson now.) He drove me to the hospital, which had a high chimney – it looked like a big cigarette – out of which a lot of smoke was pouring. I thought: my mother's dead already and they're burning her, because I had the crematorium and the hospital mixed up.

We met a doctor – an Indian woman – who held my hand as we walked down a long green corridor. The corridor smelt of food: not normal food but food that, like the people in the hospital, was really ill. We kept barging through swing doors, like cowboys bursting into one saloon after another, and then another Indian woman doctor was walking towards us. She looked just like the first one, so it looked as though the first one was walking towards a mirror, but everything was so weird that there was nothing weird about this. As she walked, the second Indian woman did a particular thing with her two hands, as if she was saying, 'Shoo, get back!', and that's exactly what she *was* saying. My mother was dead.

My uncle and aunt took me in, and, on that first night, they opened a bottle of wine because they were in shock. They were both really nice to me, and Wilkinson asked me to try some wine. It was red and I expected it to taste like cherryade; when it didn't, and when it tasted like *wine*, I said, 'It needs more sugar', making them both laugh for the first and last time during my acquaintanceship with them.

Christine's funeral was a few days later. I was not asked if I wanted to go. All I knew of it was that when I got back to my uncle's place after school the furniture was pushed back against the walls, there was a party can of Tetley's on the coffee table, and a man I didn't know was shitfaced in the corner. After that, I never saw any more alcohol in the house. The pair of them were actually teetotallers.

Wilkinson could not have children. He was a long, droopy bloke with long red ears, who rode a Honda Ninety and supported York City, and did tour-guiding as a hobby so I wasn't particularly surprised – at least, I wasn't surprised when I thought about it later. His wife – who was called Maureen and looked like Princess Anne – worked at Safeways as a cashier, and I always thought of her as Wilkinson's mother. They'd always wanted to adopt a child, and there I was. Because they were family, it went through on the nod from whoever makes the decisions about these things.

The two of them lived at the end of Chantry Row, which was a terrace of red-brick houses that suited rain and looked out of place on a sunny day. One of the houses in the terrace was a Chinese takeaway; another was a barber's that basically had the same three old men in it every day, all getting their hair cut over and over again, and then putting flat caps on, making the whole thing a waste of time.

When I first moved in, when he was still talking to me, Wilkinson used to say: 'Walk until you can get no further, then that's us', except that it wasn't just them, it was me as well, and I couldn't believe it. The place was dark; it didn't look right. To the backs of the houses were the backyards, and behind the backyards was a lane with a wide gutter down the middle and cobbles that clanged, so you felt as though you were wearing hobnail boots as you walked along it.

When I started to get spots, I was glad that Christine wasn't around to see them because they would have been such a let-down for her. When you've got brambles some people never mention them and some others never bloody well shut up about them. Maureen was in the second category – she wanted me to cover them up with brown cream that made me look like a tandoori chicken. So I hated her. Wilkinson wasn't too bad, but he was always an old man to me, part of old York, dating from the days when the steam trains made the Bar Walls black and nobody gave a damn. And his tour-guiding got to be a serious embarrassment to me. I'd be kicking about with mates around the Minster, and there'd be Wilkinson, walking past in his raincoat on a sunny day, with any number of tourists behind him, saying, 'The Chapter House is an octagonal building with a conical roof.' As if everybody couldn't see that for themselves.

Wilkinson was a reader, and he used to pass books on to me – paperbacks, mainly written by dead people, with some ridiculous price on the back: two and six. But that stopped at a certain point, and when I was nicked for the first time,

Wilkinson just said, 'Did you do it?', as if he wasn't really bothered either way, and when he found out what happened to Cameron Lacey he sighed the only real sigh I've ever heard in my life.

Three

I sat waiting for Dean in Exhibition Square next to the fountain. I'd done one line of whiz from the wrap in the glove compartment of my Volvo 240 estate – which was parked, in all its incredible uncoolness, around the corner in Gillygate.

On the other side of the square some clubbers were buying burgers from a little van that had a crooked chimney sticking out of the roof. Some of them were still dancing, like headless chickens. The little guy in the burger van had Radio York playing, and I could hear the sound of Butteridge floating over the flagstones. He was still *on*.

'I mean some o't' Yorkshire puddin's we're gettin' now . . . frankly ah've seen bigger vol au vents . . .'

'You're saying they're too small?' said the interviewer.

'Aye,' said Butteridge. *'Too small by 'alf.'*

Next to me was the BHS carrier bag with my little jemmy in it, and a torch, which was actually the front light off the Palm Beach, and in my hands was the *New Yorkshire Leader*, which I'd found on the bench, and which had Butteridge on the front page, talking about a Yorkshire-pudding-eating contest, at which he was going to be lording it as VIP judge. This solved the mystery of the night's broadcasts. I was reading the paper when Dean rolled up, slightly late.

'Wicked bobble, man,' he said.

He was talking about the hat I wear pulled down low for a job.

'Hi,' I said, standing up.

I looked at Dean; from the van I could still hear Butteridge:

25

'Well, over t'years I 'ave developed a few basic prejudices, as yer might say, about what I will and will not tolerate in t'Yorkshire puddin's that are served up for me by t'wife. Number one . . .'

'I fink it's starting to rain,' said Dean.

I explained that this was just the spray from the fountain.

'Oh,' said Dean, 'right.'

'There's a bit in here about Bryan Butteridge,' I said, shoving the *Leader* over to him.

Dean looked a bit baffled.

'He's the TV guy,' I reminded him, 'the mark.'

(I was using what I thought might be Dean's terminology.)

'Aw,' Dean said, nodding but still not taking the paper off me, 'Kit Butteridge.'

It was interesting that he said that. Dean was like the straw man in *The Wizard of Oz*. No brain. But say the word 'Butteridge', even to him, and you got back 'Kit'.

Kit Butteridge was Bryan's old man, and he was the original and best. Bryan was on the front page of the *New Yorkshire Leader* roughly every day but rarely made the national papers. The show *Wayfarin'*, by contrast, had made his dad into a megastar. As a kid I'd watch the repeats of those black-and-white shows, with Kit tramping across fields and just . . . spouting, making it up as he went along. You couldn't believe it wasn't bullshit, but it actually wasn't, and even now, when some clip from *Wayfarin'* is shown, it'll be introduced by a Yorkshire star of the present day (Parkinson or Hattersley, or some clown like that) pointing out how good it was. Kit had class in other words; he was a top bloke, so it was weird that he called his son Bryan.

I was still holding the *Leader* out to Dean, but he was just standing in front of me, looking away from it, and that's when I clicked. I lobbed the paper into a bin.

'Let's go,' I said, feeling odd.

We walked under Bootham Bar.

'Bill's a lovely geezer, don't you fink?' said Dean. 'But one fing . . . he's never done bird has he?'

'That's right,' I said. 'He's a very smart guy.'

'Vat uvver guy . . . Walter . . . he's all right, innee?'

'No,' I said.

'I like ver guy, but what's his track record?'

'He's done YOI,' I said. 'Burglary and dealing.'

'He's a hard man, don't you fink?'

'He's a fucking headcase, if that's what you mean.'

'Done time yourself, have you?' I said to Dean.

'I've done YOI,' said Dean, 'and I was five mumfs on remand in Brixton.'

'Charge?'

'Dealing.'

'Dealing in what?'

'Amphetamime.' (That's what he said; not 'amphetamine'.)

'But you got off.'

Dean nodded.

'Bit of a result, actually.'

I liked the way he wasn't swell-headed about being charged or about getting off.

As we walked through empty York, I watched Dean move. It was quite funny because he had a strutting sort of step but with a tremble built in, so he was like a cross between a very old guy and a very young guy.

'How do you know Bill?' I said, just to see what he'd say.

'Friend of a friend,' said Dean. 'I was just telling him about Reggie and Ronnie Kray.'

'The Krays?' I said. 'That's going back a bit.'

'But ver legend lives on. Vey were such diamonds ver pair of 'em . . . wouldn't harm a fly.'

27

'But didn't Ronnie Kray used to cut people's faces off?'

'Well yeah,' said Dean, tripping over a bit of wonky pavement, 'but . . .'

The Minster was looming up, and you *can't* ignore it actually, so I sort of tipped my head in its direction, doing my tourist guide bit, and Dean did look at the Minster for quite a time as we tracked past.

'What do you think?' I asked.

'Yeah,' said Dean. He was quiet for a while and then he said: 'Vey've got a church like vat in Leytonstone.'

We turned into Butteridge's street, which was just behind the Minster, a secret sort of street, tucked away, enviable in the extreme. The houses had originally belonged to church bosses – canons maybe, I don't really know. They had big gardens, and two of them had greenhouses the size of bungalows. In amongst the gardens were ruins of buildings more ancient than the Minster, and Butteridge's house was guarded by some sort of old tollbooth. Thinking about it, I'd seen it on a postcard.

At 3.15 a.m. the two of us stood there with this thing between us and Bryan Butteridge's long front garden. The buzz, as usual, was incredible, so much so that in a way you didn't want to get the job done because then it would be over, and you'd be back to square one.

I put my gloves on.

'What's in ver bag?' said Dean, as we ducked into the front garden.

I held open the carrier for him to see the stuff.

'Cor, well tooled up you are!' he said.

Actually, I was travelling light, and Dean himself didn't seem to have brought anything at all to the party, except his loud bloody voice.

'Haven't you got any gloves?' I said.

'No,' he said, 'I didn't fink.'

28

'But they've got your prints?'

'Ver law's got 'em, yeah.'

'Roll your sleeves right down,' I said.

Dean rolled the sleeves of his West Ham shirt down, but he didn't do it very *well*.

'Look,' I said, 'don't touch anything, OK? Just watch. You're not carrying, are you?'

'A fucking shooter, you mean?'

'Anyfing.'

Bloody hell, I was catching Dean's disease.

'Any*thing*,' I said.

Dean shook his head, making me feel like a wanker for getting heavy with him although he hadn't seemed too bothered. He was a very strange sort of bloke; very innocent seeming.

Butteridge lived in a tall, black tower of a house, and the front of it was rounded like the back of a boat – the stern. Next to the front door was a blue plaque saying Kit Butteridge lived here blah blah blah – no mention of Bryan, funnily enough. I walked up to the letterbox and clattered it; Dean nodded at me, and we waited, ready to make for the Volvo, although nothing was going to stop me going into that house on that night because it was my big chance of a comeback after YOI.

Hearing nothing at all, we headed for the right side of the house. Squeezed between the Butteridge mansion and the one next door was a sort of wooden lean-to. It had a basic wooden door, which wobbled open when I touched the handle. Inside was a green filing cabinet, a busted cardboard box full of mouldy books and two dustbins, but the target was the side door of the main house.

I could feel the sweat streaming off me – fleeing the scene of the crime, so to speak – as I took the jemmy out of the bag and crammed a red liquorice into my mouth. I always eat red liquorice on a job. It brings me luck you see, although in fact it doesn't.

Dean started eyeballing me.

'Do you want a piece?' I asked, pissed off.

'What is it?' said Dean.

'Red liquorice,' I said.

'What?' said Dean, who couldn't hear me because my mouth was full of the stuff.

'Red liquorice,' I said again after a while. 'Do you want some?'

'No fanks, mate,' said Dean.

I took the jemmy out, and Dean started panting 'little jemmy, yeah, lovely little jemmy', as if he was talking about a person called 'little Jenny'.

I whacked it into the crack, and started levering; I was totally *on* it.

'Go on, my son!' said Dean.

I let this go, and carried on working with the jemmy.

'Vet's ver boy!' said Dean. 'Give it some fucking elbow, go on!'

'Will you fucking well shut up?' I said.

'Aw,' said Dean, 'sorry, mate.'

But he'd put my pressure up to exploding point. I worked away for two minutes, and then I'd had enough, so I stood up and rammed the jemmy through one of the little panes of old glass at the top of the door. That bit of glass had been green; next I did a red one; then I crouched down next to Dean, shaking.

'Why did you do vat?' he said, after a while.

'Because I'm fucking pissed off,' I said.

I was pissed off with Butteridge for having a decent lock on his door, and I was pissed off with myself for smashing the glass, which was totally unprofessional.

'Shall I tell you what I fink?' said Dean.

'No,' I said.

A few seconds went by – nothing happened.

'OK,' I said to Dean, 'what do you think?'

'Ver first fing', said Dean, not all that promisingly, as he stood up and leant against Butteridge's door, 'is . . .'

As Dean Martin fell into Bryan Butteridge's house I realized that I *had* opened the door after all.

I left my jemmy on the doorstep and walked in.

The kitchen was done in a country style, and it was sort of faded. It smelt of old bananas. Near the door was a swivel-top bin with a little parade of beer cans alongside – Bimmington's Bog Standard. The next room – Dean was already in it with my torch – was the living room. Two flowery patterned sofas with frilly edges . . . some little round fancy tables . . . pink and yellow dried flowers in the fireplace. The mantelpiece was packed with pot animals, and the carpet was pink and yellow and totally disgusting.

But the paintings on the wall didn't fit in. There was no sign of Little Bo Peep, or a horse, or any such nonsense. Instead there were just shapes: squares and circles and that kind of thing. Geometric stuff; abstracts or whatever. I looked at the VCR under the massive Sanyo TV, thinking it would be so simple just to take that and go.

Dean went into the hallway, and I noticed half-a-dozen copies of some new book that had two titles. It was called *The Yorkshire Dales: A Coffee Table Book*, but it was also called *The Ever Changing Seasons of The Yorkshire Dales – A Pictorial Essay by Phil Spalding with an Introduction by Bryan Butteridge*. On the cover was a tree in a snowdrift, and on the jacket flap were the mug shots and potted biographies, so I read Butteridge's.

'Bryan Butteridge', it said, 'is familiar across God's Own

County and beyond as the son of the late, great writer, broadcaster and Yorkshireman, Kit Butteridge. Bryan has followed in the footsteps of his father with a series of writings and TV programmes on the lives of ordinary Yorkshire folk. Every week in his long-running TV series, *Rambling with Bryan Butteridge*, Bryan meets the fascinating local characters of the Broad Acres, and evokes the ever-changing moods of their natural environment.

'Bryan lives in North Yorkshire with his wife, Angela, who is famous from his works as "t'finest lass in t'land". Bryan's hobbies are drinking real ale, shove 'apenny, and preserving the cultural heritage of Northern England – in that order. He holds a degree in history from Sheffield University.'

And he is a wanker, I thought.

I stepped into the hall, where a standard lamp was shining on Dean Martin. He was engaged in sitting at the bottom of the staircase looking at some pictures of naked ladies in a jazz mag.

'Vis guy's a dirty bastard,' he said, standing up, and showing me the jazz mag.

'Where did you find it?' I said.

'In vat coat,' he said, pointing at a brown thing hanging near the front door.

Then – and you could almost see the guy thinking – Dean walked across the hall, and put the coat on. It did not transform him into a country-gentleman-type person.

There was a mirror in the hall, and I started looking into it for some reason.

I look like a puppet, I think – Pinocchio. My face is always brownish, and I've got a turned-up nose that takes me by surprise if I ever see it from the side, reflected in one mirror that's reflecting into another or whatever. I'd lost a lot of weight, because in YOI you do everything 'on the double', and there were the leftovers of two brambles on my jaw . . . but you're so made up when they've gone that you don't mind the horrible scabs they leave behind.

'Quick shufty?' said Dean, shoving the jazz mag into the pocket of the coat and pointing up the staircase.

I didn't like this, but I followed him up the stairs and saw two pictures propped against the walls: the horse, and Little Bo Peep, or at any rate some kind of little fairy glowing on a hill.

'Sorted!' yelled Dean, which is when I heard the voices.

Somebody was coming through a door, so I pulled Dean into the nearest room, which had in it one bed, a bedside table, a jug and sod all else. The moonlight through the window was making everything light grey as I heard a man, not Butteridge but a southerner, saying: 'She said, and I quote, "The very title *Rambling with Bryan Butteridge* implies a lack of editorial stringency." You know my answer, Bry, and I've said it for years – you change one letter.'

'You mean the old idea of calling it *Ramblin'* with 'n' apostrophe?' (This was Bryan Butteridge, using his ordinary voice.)

'No, Bry,' said the southerner, 'try going to the other end.'

'Eh?' said Butteridge.

'Ambling *with Bryan Butteridge*,' said the southerner, very pleased with himself. 'Do that, and you'll rejuvenate the whole concept.'

'*Over mah dead body,*' said Butteridge.

'"Ambling" captures it all,' said the southerner, 'your tough lyricism, your native wit, your rough-hewn natural charm.'

'Bollocks,' said Butteridge.

'I hate to say it, Bry, but we've got to lose the song request.'

'Fuck off.'

'It doesn't work, Bry. How many more times are you going to have to play "I Will Always Love You" by Whitney Houston? And it's not original. I mean, it's far too *Down Your*

Way, far too *Desert Island Discs.*'

'Yeah, but *Rambling* was the first show to do it *after Down Your Way* and *Desert Island Discs.*'

'Well, I think you should have a word with Foot, Bry, try to reason with her. She's from the north herself, I believe.'

'Where?' said Butteridge.

'Birmingham.'

'BIRMINGHAM!' yelled Butteridge from inside the room. The southerner had been walking towards the door, but now he stopped dead.

'What's the problem, Bry?' he said, turning around.

'Fucking *Birmingham*!' said Butteridge.

'What about it?'

'It's *not* in the north.'

'Well, where the hell is it then?'

'It's in the Midlands, which is in the fucking *south* of England, all right? It's not in the north! Yorkshire is in the north! This place, this bloody city . . .'

There was a great kerfuffle inside the room – I couldn't interpret it.

'Everything I know is in the north,' Butteridge was saying, when I could hear him again, 'and I am in the north and the programmes that I make are in the north, and Alison sodding Foot is in the south, and she does not understand, and never the twain shall meet.'

'So you won't see her for lunch then?'

'Yes,' said Butteridge, now very quiet. 'I suppose I probably will do.'

The southerner walked across the hallway and into the lav. He did a slash, came back out and stood still for a second, letting me see that he was a small, shiny bloke in a good suit.

'Bry,' he said, walking back towards the open door, 'we're fighting for our lives here. There's a new programme about the north starting in a fortnight. It's presented by Jed Thorpe. You're familiar with his work, presumably?'

'He's never done any bloody work has he?'

'I mean his music. His new album, *We Are The New North* is being hailed by the critics as the greatest thing ever to come out of Cackheaton.'

'*Cleck*heaton,' said Butteridge.

'Whatever,' said the southerner.

I could hear the ring top being pulled off a can – had to be a beer can. Then one of the two – most likely Butteridge – let rip with an almighty belch.

'Actually,' said Butteridge, who was obviously bladdered, 'Roger Hargreaves is the greatest thing ever to come out of Cleckheaton.'

'Who's he?' said the southerner.

'Wrote the Mr Men books for children. *Ah've read t'lot of 'em and they're fuckin' knockout ah'll tell yer.*'

'Well, I'm not going to argue the toss on this one,' said the southerner, 'but you should know that Thorpe has got a very distinctive vocal style due to the fact that he sings with chewing-gum in his mouth, which is apparently very dangerous because he could easily swallow it and choke to death at any time.'

'That'd be good,' said Butteridge, quiet again.

There was a bit of muttering between the two of them, then I heard the southerner saying: 'Chin up, Bry. You've had your setbacks in the past. Remember *Hull: A Coffee Table Book*? That did nothing, Bry, not even in Hull, but you bounced straight back with your introduction to Knaresborough for the *Pub to Pub* series – a really stunning piece of work. And I was reading *The Yorkshire Dales: A Coffee Table Book* on the way up, which looks great. Where do you think the muse will be taking you next, Bry?'

'*The Yorkshire Wolds: A Coffee Table Book,*' said Butteridge, sounding incredibly pissed off.

'Sounds like another biggie,' said the southerner. 'Look, I've got to turn in, Bry. I'm on the seven thirty going back.'

A bit more muttering from the two of them. Then I noticed that Dean was asleep on the fucking bed. Next to him was a cat that I hadn't seen before. It was asleep as well.

The room we were in was mainly full of books by old Kit Butteridge. I picked up *Platform Nine, Barnsley Station* and read the famous first line: 'It was raining in Barnsley but there was nothing new about that.' This book, written in 1957, was a classic but I hadn't read it so I shoved it down the front of my pants.

Kit Butteridge had written more than I thought, including *How To Watch Birds; The Coast Around Scarborough – A Geological Summary; Flora and Fauna of the North Yorks Coast – with over 500 Illustrations; Kit Butteridge's Yorkshire Question and Answer Book for Children* – all kinds of things. In most of the books there was a photograph of Kit, who was always wearing a sort of Robin Hood hat with a feather in it.

Looking at those shots, I thought about the time before I went bad and just before old Kit died, when he made a visit to the Grammar, and I sat at his feet in my role as 'top in first-year English' (but bloody useless at everything else). Afterwards, he ruffled my hair and I wanted to follow him out of the door because when Kit Butteridge ruffled your hair it *stayed* ruffled.

I'd liked the look of him then, but his face in these books . . . it looked as though it was made out of stone: he looked a nasty bastard actually.

There were also a lot of books by other dead people: books on art, books on wood carving, a *lot* of books on furniture. And propped on top of the main bookshelf was a picture – I couldn't tell whether it was a photograph or a drawing – of a strange-looking table with the leg measurements and other funny little notes scrawled all around it.

Then I heard a new noise. Looking through the chink I saw the little southerner creaking upstairs on to the third floor while Butteridge stayed in the room the two of them had been talking in. As soon as he'd gone Butteridge did an incredibly loud fart that woke Dean up.

'What vee hell was vat?' he said.

'It was a fart,' I said, 'by Bryan Butteridge.'

'Who?' said Dean.

Then the niff came through to us.

'Vat is fucking out of order,' said Dean, shaking his head.

After maybe ten minutes, Butteridge came out of the room, turned off the light and walked up to the third floor, following the shiny bloke. When he'd gone we moved to the top of the stairs and saw that the paintings were still there, next to the toilet door, which was open.

I was just about to grab the pictures when I clicked to the fact that Dean was standing at the bog and actually pissing into it. I could not believe what I was seeing.

'Cut it out, you fucking idiot,' I whispered.

'Can't stop in ver middle,' said Dean.

That piss went on for longer than any other piss I've ever heard, and it was all being picked up by a microphone that somebody had shoved down the bog – at least that's what it sounded like.

'All vat Yorkshire beer,' said Dean, finally turning around and putting his bloody dick away.

'Let's get out of here,' I said.

'Right,' said Dean, and he flushed the chain.

As Butteridge thundered down on us screaming 'Buggeration!' while holding in his hand a fucking *gun*, Dean Martin reeled out of the bog and, as he swivelled toward the stair-case, I saw a glimmer of something steely in his hand – a blade. The situation was totally out of control, but Dean didn't cut Butteridge; he just sort of half fell and half ran downstairs yelling out, 'Where's yer fucking way out?' – because basically he'd forgotten.

I was coming down the stairs after Dean screaming at Butteridge, 'Point that fucking thing at me and I'll have my fucking solicitor on you, you fucking *nonce*.'

But then I skidded on a rag rug, and everything went a bit funny.

'I want a word with you,' Butteridge was slowly saying, quite an odd little woozy while later. 'I have a gun . . .'

I could see that – it was a revolver. He also had his ridiculous fucking Chelsea boot on my throat. I wasn't scared of being shot by a clown like Butteridge. I was more scared of Neville, and I didn't even know whether he existed. I was watching a spider walk across the hall floor, and thinking . . . five . . . I'll go away for five years this time, which was fine, except there were some new pictures in my mind that made me feel sad about the idea of going back inside: Bill's house, lit up like a lantern; Bill's gorgeous wife, looking at me, and even Dean Martin looking into my carrier bag and saying, 'Cor, well tooled up you are!' The downside, as usual, had been Walter Bowler, but mainly the evening had been a blast.

'Listen, son,' said Bryan Butteridge, bending down over me, reeking of real ale, and moving his horrible, shagged-out, famous face close to mine, 'Listen to me . . .'

Four

After Christine died I used to sit trying to imagine a man on a bike pedalling along a straight, clear road and not having a crash or falling off, and I just could not do it. I'd started to think that everything ended in disaster so I thought: fine, bring it on.

The first house that I did was on the estate that Cameron Lacey lived on, and he came with me although he didn't really want to.

I'd been in Lacey's class at school since age four. They kept the Eleven Plus longer in York than most places, and we both passed it, which was a bit more of a surprise with me than him. Lacey was a bright kid who had a way with words. He said that when his mother shouted up to him the news that he'd be going to Bishy Grammar and not the Secondary Modern, he was sitting on the toilet, and 'the good news relieved that moment of pain when the turd comes out of your arse'.

Christine used to say how pretty he was. Once, when he had mumps, we went around to see him, and I can remember her stroking Lacey's swollen neck and saying, over and over again, 'so lush', which was embarrassing because to me he looked like the Elephant Man.

Like me (until the crash) Lacey was brought up by his mother. His parents had split up, but his dad was still around. Lacey's old man was a flashy bloke who always seemed to be wearing sunglasses and drove around York in a 1973 Ford Capri that was in perfect condition. Behind it, he pulled a speedboat on a trailer.

I didn't know he was dodgy, of course, but the shades would have been a clue. He also liked a bet, and he liked a drink. One Boxing Day he took Lacey and myself to Wetherby Races. There was snow on the ground, and Lacey's dad was wearing a fur coat and drinking lagers from plastic glasses. Every race, the horses went past twice in a cloud of steam, and each time it happened Lacey's dad was that bit more pissed, to the point where he was wanting to buy *us* beers.

He started putting his arm around Lacey, and I thought, so this is how it looks: father and son. It seemed like a novelty act to me; it certainly didn't look very likely to last, and a couple of weeks after that Lacey's old man cleared off for good. Sometimes it's disappointing that there aren't more surprises in this life.

Lacey's mother was very different: clever (she'd been to university) and yet she had no money . . . I couldn't get my head round that one. I knew she had no money because she lived with Lacey in half a house; in London you'd call it a flat with no problem, but in York the term's not really used.

She smoked roll-ups and never wore any make-up. I would stare at her, trying to imagine some way in which you could look at her and think: yes, she's pretty, but I never could, which drove me half mad. I once told her that she should grow her hair, and she said, 'What the fuck do you know?' In a funny way though, I fancied her, because whenever she started talking, I didn't want her to stop.

Lacey was always a gricer – a trainspotter, I mean, but he took the piss out of himself for being into trains, so you didn't really mind. He knew all the history. He knew the difference between the North Eastern Railway Company and the London and North Eastern Railway Company, and he would *tell* you. You wouldn't be listening, but he'd tell you – it was just something he had to get off his chest.

Obviously, like any gricer, he liked the steam trains better. The modern trains, the little electrical ones that look as though they've got two back ends, he could take or leave. 'Fucking Sprinter,' he'd say. 'Fucking Networker.' But he still knew all about them.

I'd go to the station with him, and I still liked it in those days because it reminded me of good times with Christine. I was never a gricer myself, but Lacey and myself did have certain things in common: rum and black, for example – that was our drink, because one day I suddenly remembered that it had been Christine's drink.

We also both read everything by Terry Pratchett, although I kept bloody quiet about it. It was the guy's hat that got to me, but Lacey would say: 'It is a stupid hat, yes, but you've got to look at the guy's mind. He's totally out there in his mind.'

After reading every Terry Pratchett book – and there's about fifty of the bloody things – Lacey started writing science fiction for himself, even inventing this planet that had a name beginning with (guess what?) Z.

'Why do all planets in sci-fi have to begin with fucking Z?' I asked him. 'Just make up a planet beginning with something else, like a D for instance, and you'd be totally unique.'

He went very quiet when I said that because he really prided himself on his writing, and he knew I was right – there was quite a lot of respect between us, even though Lacey was in the Sea Cadets . . .

This was the weirdest thing of all. I mean he was literally *in* the Sea Cadets, and he went off every Tuesday or whatever it was to the SS *Eileen* which was a disused warehouse in Toft Green that was pretending to be a boat. He was also a child star of the York Mystery Plays, which are outdoor performances held, in the rain, for tourists in the Museum Garden. He played the part of a messenger of some sort, in a pink dress, tights and pixie boots. I gave him endless amounts of stick about this but I can still recite the three lines he had.

So Lacey would have all these ludicrous hobbies, and I'd sort of watch him have them, with one exception: BMX.

We were very heavily into that, but the atmosphere in York was wrong for BMX, basically because it wasn't an urban wasteland. When you're twelve years old, and you're growing up in York, you wish the place was more like Brixton. If you're twelve years old growing up in Brixton, I dare say it's the other way around, but you'd probably keep quiet about it because York's not cool and Brixton is.

We got involved in a campaign to have a half-pipe built in York, and that was the first time we appeared in the *New Yorkshire Leader* – Lacey, me, and about four other Yorkie slackers riding our bikes in our Bermudas and bowling shirts, 'getting air', calling each other 'man', and smoking spliff, which is very much part of the teenage BMX scene (along with wanking around the clock, although nobody talks about that very much).

The second time we appeared in the *Leader*, we didn't actually *appear*. Underneath the words 'THEIR NAMES LIVETH FOR EVER MORE' on the War Memorial in Station Road we spray-painted 'Baz Carter', who'd just come to York City on a free transfer from Cardiff. I thought it was funny because there was no way Baz Carter was going to make the first team. I think it's funny to this day, although it was obviously a totally mindless action. The *Leader* took a picture, and a York vicar wrote an article on what we'd done – three-quarters of a page of incredible stodge that I read out loud to Lacey. They had a quote in there from Baz Carter himself: 'I totally disassociate myself from this stupid prank.'

'The word', said Lacey, 'is dissociate' – a pretty cool response, I thought.

42

Our little adventures were gradually getting a bit more iffy, and, although Lacey was into the buzz of what we were doing, I was the one who kept us at it, looking for the big breakthrough: that first house.

Five

Like every Yorkie, I'd seen Butteridge in person before, but never this close.

Basically, his hair and beard were grey; his eyebrows were black and grey. His eyes were grey and blue, and his face was grey. He wasn't fat and he wasn't thin. He was wearing a thin jacket of the kind I've seen many times on blokes selling tickets for deckchairs, cords that were too short for him, and Chelsea boots with elasticated sides; and he was going bald, which you wouldn't know looking at the pictures of him in his crap books. Up close you could actually see the head under the hair.

I was standing next to the window in the room in which he'd been talking to the southerner. It had dark wood walls and a blue carpet. Everywhere were stacks of cardboard folders. There was an old-fashioned computer (I mean, a bloody *Amstrad*, steam-powered) with a sticker on the side that said 'Campaign For Real Ale 1997 Yorkshire Booze Cruise'. On the wall was a brownish map with the words 'North Yorkshire' written in fancy print right across it.

Butteridge was holding two cans of Bimmington's in one hand. If he was still packing the revolver, I couldn't see it any more.

'I saw your fucking crowbar,' he said. 'In the kitchen. Why'd you leave it there?'

'You don't want to carry a weapon,' I said, taking out my packet of Silk Cut, then putting them back in my pocket when I saw that my hand was shaking. 'You might use it.'

I took the Silkies out again because my hands had stopped shaking.

'Feel free to smoke,' said Butteridge, being sarcastic.

Butteridge poured the beers at his desk, then said, 'Watch', and walked over to the window. He pulled the six-shooter out of his jacket pocket and threw it into his dark back garden. I immediately thought about scarpering but I really wanted to know what he was going to say next.

'The deal is . . .' he said, sitting down at his desk, 'you talk to me; I don't talk to the police.'

'That's fine,' I said, taking the Kit Butteridge book out of my underpants, because it was hurting my dick.

Butteridge didn't say anything but just stared at me for a long, long time.

'You look like fucking Noddy,' he said.

I took this as a reference to the hat.

'You've seen me on television, right?' he said.

'*Rambling*', I said, 'yeah.'

'Read some of the stuff I've written?'

'I've read some of your dad's stuff.'

He didn't like that one bit.

'*Bollocks to 'im*, what about mine?'

'*The Yorkshire Dales: A Coffee Table Book*,' I said. 'I was looking at that downstairs.'

'What did you think?'

I shrugged.

'You're a literary purist, aren't you?' said Butteridge, sitting back and pointing at the Kit Butteridge book that I'd just taken out of my pants. 'An appreciator of fine writing who can't pretend to like anything else, even for the sake of making amends to the poor sod whose house he's just broken into, wrecking the kitchen door in the process. Why'd you have to smash the glass?'

I just shrugged again.

'Slipped,' I said.

'It'll cost a fortune to replace. Fucking listed, this house is.'

'Does that mean it's falling over?' I said.

'Oh,' said Butteridge, 'I'm killing myself laughing at that one.'

He seemed pissed off, but not very.

'Literary purists,' he said, looking away from me and scratching his hair, 'funny how they crop up all over the place.'

'Do you always write just introductions?' I said, trying to rile him somewhat.

'Not *just* introductions,' said Butteridge, reaching for an Embassy Regal. 'Prefaces – I do a few of those, and I've branched out into forewords lately. People think a TV name's going to sell their book, you see.'

After lighting his cigarette, he started eyeballing me again. If he was trying to freak me out he wasn't having much success. I mean, he wasn't exactly *Neville*; he wasn't even Walter Bowler.

'What did you want to talk to me about?' I said.

'I wish you'd take that bloody hat off,' he said.

He took three quick drags on his Regal, then carried on.

'They're dropping my TV show, or changing it beyond recognition. There's a new woman at the BBC called Alison Foot, who's twenty-eight and thinks I'm past it. She's just come over from pop music, where she completely revitalized *Juke Box Jury*.'

Butteridge folded his arms and looked at me as though he was interviewing me for a job, waiting for me to say something clever.

I looked down at the floor.

'You mean to say you've not noticed this revitalization?' he said.

'I don't watch that shite,' I said.

'*But you're a young feller,*' said Butteridge, getting agitated again, '*you're t'fuckin' target audience.*'

He stood up, crashed his Regal into the ashtray.

'Wait,' he said, and he was gone.

The first thing I looked at was the copper ashtray. It was as big as a dinner plate and, underneath the crushed Embassy butts of Bryan Butteridge was written: 'Presented to Kit Butteridge, Pipeman of the Year 1978'. On the desk next to the word processor was a letter from somebody called Mary Dougal of 'Ebor Yorkshire Pudding Oven Trays Inc.'

'Dear Mr Butteridge,' Mary Dougal had typed (badly) 'many thanks again for agreeing to do the honours at the Tenth Annual Ebor Yorkshire Pudding Oven Trays Yorkshire Pudding Eating Contest, and associated promotional work. I'm sorry that the fee is not in line with your expectations, but my managing director has assured your agent that if all goes well this time around, we will look at the possibility of reviewing our terms for next year. Please find enclosed a copy of the rules.'

On the second sheet of paper I read: 'Rule Number One: The winner of the Tenth Annual Ebor Yorkshire Pudding Oven Trays Yorkshire Pudding Eating Contest shall be the person who, in the alloted time, eats the most Yorkshire puddings.'

There were no other rules.

Underneath this stuff was a paper headed 'Inland Revenue, Self-Assessment – Statement of Account'. There were a lot of figures but one stood out above all others: 'Balance of Account,' I read, '54,912.85. Please pay the overdue amount now.' It freaked me out I have to say, and it wasn't even my bill.

I walked around the walls, looking at the pictures: old photographs of the north, and one framed photo of Kit Butteridge and some others. It was taken from a newspaper and, underneath, it said: 'From left to right: Kit Butteridge, OBE, FRS, MA, LLD, J. B. Priestley, OM, MA, Litt.D., LLD, D.Litt., and the Rt Hon. Sir Harold Wilson, KG, PC, OBE, FRS, share a joke after the presentations.' The three of them were wearing gowns, and J. B. Priestley – the only one I hadn't actually been able to put a name to – was smoking his pipe.

Next to this was a shot of Bryan Butteridge. He was shaking hands with the northern comedians, Sid Little and Eddie Large. They were in a funfair, standing alongside a clown on stilts, and some scrawly writing underneath said: 'Bry, Sid and Eddie, Joe Corrigan's Funfair, Scarborough, 1985 . . . By, we'll sup some stuff toneet!'

Butteridge walked back into the room.

'*Aye*,' he said (he'd gone full on again, for some reason), *''ave a good look. Tek yer time, and when yer done 'ave a geg at this.'*

I sat down and Butteridge did the same. He handed over a book called *British Furniture in the Twentieth Century*, and, as he puffed and blew on another Regal, I read the bit he'd marked out in pencil.

'Perhaps the most important member of this obscure group of Yorkshire Modernists', I read, 'was Edward Johns (1880–1915). His Chair Number One in bent and laminated birch is one of the earliest examples of functionalism in chair-making. It is rigorous in the extreme, spurning any decorative embellishment, and forms a dining set with his equally austere Table Number One (see fig. 12). Towards the end of his short and sparsely documented life, Johns produced his Chair Number Two which, whilst also strikingly original, was both less finely balanced and more conventional in appearance than Chair Number One.'

When I'd finished reading this nonsense, Butteridge leant forwards and turned the pages of the book for me until he reached fig. 12. There was the chair: Chair Number One. It looked strange.

Now Butteridge looked at me for another long time, before standing up again and saying, 'Follow me', in a way that had me thinking: does he fancy my ring or what? He lead me into his basement where the bricks were crumbly and black. He turned on the light, and there, underneath the swinging bulb, was a table that looked like the chair that had been in the book.

The chair in the book had looked to be made of a lot of planks nailed together – there was no cushion involved. One of the planks, standing on its end, made what would've been two of the legs of any normal sort of chair; the other two legs were made by one curved piece of wood which came out of the side of the chair and reminded me of the wheel on a paddle steamer, or the big claw of a lobster.

The same idea was behind the table in the basement – everything about it was extremely straight or extremely curved, I mean. The top of it had the same outline as an egg sitting in a square egg cup. Underneath the egg-cup end was a double wooden arch, like the McDonald's sign, while the other end of the table was held up by just one plank, making a total of four legs in all: three at one end and one (thick one) at the other, if that makes any sense.

'You saw those paintings in the living room?' said Butteridge.

I nodded.

'They were my old man's – not my taste at all, and the wife bloody hates them. You wouldn't think it, but he was into modern art, and this table comes under that heading. He came across it in Leeds covered market,' said Butteridge, sitting down on top of the table, and running his hands all over it. 'When he found out what it was he spent ten years looking for the chairs.'

'Did he think they might be valuable?' I said, sitting down on the cellar stairs.

'No, he was just doing it for a laugh.'

Butteridge lolled right across the top of the table, as if he was a gorgeous model in a centrefold, and started talking to the basement ceiling.

'In Germany,' he said, 'they rate Edward Johns higher than anybody in the entire world – the entire world of furniture-making, I mean, because they think he inspired the Bauhaus movement. Are you with me?'

I wasn't; but then again I sort of *was*. I didn't say anything though. I thought it best to just smoke.

'When the old man snuffed it,' said Butteridge, still looking up to the ceiling of his basement, 'I started doing some digging myself. Then I got lucky . . .'

And that's when the whole story came out.

By 5 a.m. we were back in his workroom, with me drinking from a can of Bimmington's Bog Standard, and Butteridge downing a selection box of Scotch miniatures, sometimes unfolding the little tickets that came with the bottles and reading out, in a pissed voice, 'The Llanleekie Malt gains its distinctive savour from the crystal clear springs of Dunscroggie.' And things like that.

Butteridge started by talking about his house: he'd inherited it from his old man and it was now double-mortgaged, if that's the right term. He was in debt up to his bloody ears at any rate, and the bottom line was this: the chairs made by Edward Johns to go with Table Number One were in a museum on the North Yorkshire Moors that I'd never heard of and that was called 'Mr Ollernshaw's House'. Here, they were used as back-up chairs when the tea room was over-crowded, which wasn't all that often.

At Mr Ollernshaw's House, nobody knew what the chairs

were, but they were not for sale (Butteridge knew that because he'd tried to buy them), and therefore they had to be nicked. At a party in Hebden Bridge, Bryan Butteridge had met a half-German, half-American dodgy gay millionaire antique-dealer who was willing to pay a lot of money for the table and chairs together.

There were four chairs, and they were quite big, so what was needed was a gang of four. These four would operate in the time frame between the night alarms being switched off by some old biddy who did the cleaning, and the arrival of the rest of the museum people.

Only towards six o'clock, when the southerner – who was Butteridge's money man, agent or whatever, and who was called Allan Darnell – was threatening to reappear did Butteridge get into talking about hard cash. We were back in his study, with birds making an incredible racket outside, as Butteridge told me that half a million pounds was what 'the Yank' (which is what Butteridge called his Hebden Bridge contact) was willing to pay, of which Butteridge himself wanted a hundred grand for the tax bill and to get himself generally sorted financially.

I stopped Butteridge at this point and asked him why, if he was so broke, he had bought expensive paintings of Little Bo Peep and a horse, and he told me that it was his wife Angela – 't'finest lass in t'land' – who'd bought the paintings, earning herself a sound bollocking for doing so. In a strop she'd then gone off to her mother's house in Harrogate. The other £400,000, Butteridge told me, throwing the little whisky bottles one by one into the wastepaper bin in the corner of his workroom, could be split between the four people who did the chair lift.

Basically, I didn't believe a fucking word of it.

Six

One of the reasons I'd been nonce-ish about doing the Butteridge place was that I was still on licence, which meant that every week I was taken to the Danish Kitchen in Petergate and bought open-topped sandwiches by my probation officer who was a strange woman called Chalker. She was supposed to be trying to get me on a course to do A levels at York Tech, but the rest of the time she just made small talk, and I do mean *small*.

When I went to see her on the Monday after Butteridge, I was told that Sainsbury's apple juice was 20p cheaper than some other brand of apple juice; that (still on the subject of apples) she'd eaten a lot of them when she was pregnant; that, the Saturday before, she'd been to her sister's wedding in Bishops Stortford, which was not far from Luton, and that her new tumble drier had a fluffer whereas the old one did not. Or vice versa.

As she talked, I smoked Silk Cuts and worried. Bill had heard all about what had gone on at Butteridge's from Dean, and I'd given him my own version over the mobile, leaving out the stuff about the chairs (I would've looked a flake for hearing Butteridge out, and even more flaky for passing on what I'd heard), but now Bill wanted to talk to me in person. Basically, this was the first time I'd let him down, and I wasn't sure how he was going to take it. I *was* pretty sure what Bowler was going to say, though, and I was about right.

'I hear you very unexpectedly fucked up,' he said, as I walked up to where he was sitting in the Museum Gardens with Bill.

It was three o'clock, incredibly sunny, and Bill and Bowler were on a bench opposite the ruins of St Mary's Abbey. A peacock was standing on the middle of what's left of the Abbey, in between the white stone stumps, turning around and showing its tail feathers like a fashion model for the benefit of gormless tourists. But Bill and Bowler weren't watching the bird.

Bill was reading the sports section of a paper – *The Times* – with his Raybans resting in his thick grey hair.

Bowler was next to him, sweating, with the drops leaving little tracks down the side of his Spacehopper head, actually cleaning the orangey skin as they rolled. He was eating a king-sized pork pie and throwing bits to some birds that were hopping around the bench: one pigeon and half-a-dozen evil-looking crows. Whenever the pigeon came near he tried to kick it. He only liked the crows.

'Butteridge pulled a gun on me,' I said.

'Yeah?' said Bill, not even looking up from *The Times*.

Then the pigeon came a bit too close to one of Bowler's boots.

'Fuck off out of it, you twat,' he said.

'What sort of gun was it?' said Bill, still reading the paper.

'How do you mean? It was a pistol.'

'Was it a six-shooter or a semi-automatic?'

'It was a six-shooter.'

There was plenty of room on the bench but nobody was asking me to sit down.

'When he pointed it at you,' said Bill, finally folding up his paper, 'did he cock it?'

'I don't think so,' I said.

'Probably because it was a fucking water pistol,' said Bowler, throwing the last bits of pork pie at the crows. I didn't think they were supposed to be carnivores.

'Or a single-action,' said Bill, which put Bowler in his place. 'Pointing it at you, the guy's leaving himself wide open.'

'Wide open to what?'

'Spot of black, you tit,' said Bowler.

'You mean blackmail?' I said.

'I don't particularly like that word,' said Bill.

'Extortion, then,' I said.

Walter Bowler stood up and put his basketball head about an inch away from mine.

'Swallowed a fucking dictionary, have you?' he said. Then he sat back down again.

'I always knew his *programmes* were criminal,' said Bill, picking up his newspaper again, 'but I didn't think he'd carry a piece.'

I could've blamed Dean Martin, but you don't grass, so I was left with nothing to say, and feeling about as welcome as the pigeon that Bowler kept kicking, when three Japs walked up. They wanted Walter Bowler to take a picture of them standing in front of St Mary's Abbey, which they explained by smiles, and by pointing from their camera to themselves, then to the Abbey.

'Can't you see I'm busy?' said Bowler, who was sitting there with his hands in his pockets.

But the Japs didn't understand.

'Go and find some other mug to take your picture,' said Bowler, 'fucking Nips.'

'You've got to speak more slowly and clearly,' said Bill.

Bowler looked up at the Japs.

'*Fuck . . . off,*' he said, very slowly and clearly, but the Japs still didn't get the message.

'Take their bloody picture, for God's sake,' said Bill. 'We don't want a diplomatic incident.'

So Bowler stood up, took the camera off the first Jap, and all three of them turned and walked towards the Abbey. When they were ready to be photographed, Bowler put the camera to his eye, but didn't take the shot.

'Christ what a sight,' he said.

He put the camera back up to his eye, and took it down again.

'What's Japanese for smile?' he asked Bill.

'Hohoemi,' said Bill.

'I can't *believe* you know that,' said Bowler.

He was impressed, and so was I.

'If you didn't think I'd know it, why did you ask me?' said Bill, who was starting to do the crossword in his paper with a little betting-shop pen that he'd produced from somewhere.

It was at moments like this that I knew why I gave up JPS, and started smoking Bill's brand, and why I always wanted his respect, which I seemed to have completely lost. He was a top bloke.

'Hohoemi,' said Bowler, and the Japs did; they smiled.

Bowler took the picture, then put the camera into the pocket of his jogging bottoms, sat down and lit a fag.

This was a new one on the Japs, you could see that, and their smiles were starting to go a bit twitchy. Personally, I don't like tourists – they get in your way – but I did feel sorry for these three, choosing Bowler out of all the Yorkies available to take their daft little snapshot.

Bill looked up from his paper.

'Give it back, Walter,' he said.

'I'll *sell* it back to them,' said Bowler, who was now surrounded by the Japs.

'Give it fucking *back*,' said Bill again, and it was another of those little moments of needle between them that I always quite liked to see.

Bowler pulled the camera out of his pocket, shouted

55

'Catch!', and threw it at one of the women. She caught it, and said something to Bowler – something not nice. She was the only one with the balls to come back at him.

'Yeah, yeah, yeah,' said Bowler sitting back down on the bench when she'd finished her little incomprehensible speech, 'It's my town and I'll do what I fucking want.'

When the Japs had gone, we were all back to square one: Bowler and Bill sitting on the bench; me being a spare part.

'I'll see you later, Bill,' I said.

'Right you are,' said Bill.

'You'll let me know if anything comes up?'

No response, so maybe Bill hadn't heard. It was a nonsense remark anyway. I was just starting to drift off, back through the flowery rockeries, past the rich tourists and the Yorkies, sweating in their suits on their lunchbreaks from their ridiculous computer jobs, when Bill's mobile went.

'All right, Neville?' he said.

And I made my walk into a circle, and came back to Bill and Bowler. I just stood there, watching Bill on the phone, not caring about anything except the word that Bill had just said.

Bowler was eyeballing me.

'This is private business,' he said. 'Fuck off or I'll drop you.'

But I didn't move; I was too busy having a heart attack, because how many bent Nevilles in the world can there be?

It was hard to get the drift of what Bill was talking about – there was a lot about 'theatre tickets', which meant something else, but basically Bill just kept saying 'yes', and showing a lot of respect to this Neville.

Bowler looked at Bill and said, 'Put him on to me, will you?'

But Bill didn't. He finished the conversation and said to Bowler: 'Weird thing. Neville's coming up here.'

I know I went white.

'I wanted a word with him,' said Bowler, eyeballing Bill,

giving it loads; more heaviness between the two of them, but I wasn't thinking about that now.

'Sorry, Walt,' said Bill, 'but Neville had to go.'

'Where the fuck to?' said Bowler.

'He had to go to the bar actually, to get another drink. It was quite fucking *urgent*.'

'Next time,' said Bowler, 'put him on. All right?'

I was still just standing there, finding out what a coward I was. Already I was thinking: this place, this Museum Gardens, with the big, dead church and the big bushes with shiny dark leaves, and the shadows stretching across the bowling greens . . . it looks like nothing but an upper-class boneyard.

Bill said again: 'Neville's coming up here on a bit of business.'

I turned to my left and saw a leaning green gravestone. York is so historical these things crop up all over the place. Some of the paving stones are actually gravestones because they're just ten a penny in the city. This one had a robin hopping on top of it: green and red, the colours stood out in the sunshine. I read the word SCARED, and I thought: that's it in a nutshell, but then I looked again and saw: SACRED.

'I thought we were going down there to see *him*,' said Bowler.

Their bits of chat were coming at me from far away.

'We are,' said Bill, going back to his paper. 'He's coming up here about something else.'

Bowler asked the question for me: 'What?'

'He didn't want to say,' said Bill, 'and I didn't want to know.'

'We're talking nosebag, though?' said Bowler.

'It's not drug-related,' said Bill.

I wanted to go back in time; or at least go to sleep. As it was, I was standing completely still thinking about death.

Lacey's name is written in a book in York Crematorium, and I hope it's not just written in biro, but in fountain pen by somebody who knows copperplate. Christine is buried in a churchyard in the Wolds for some reason to do with her family. It sounds nice, but I've never seen it. Wilkinson goes out there with flowers on the back of his Honda some time around August when she died. He probably fancied her like everybody else, even though she was family.

Bowler was standing in front of me.

He gobbed on my top.

'Fucking Walter,' said Bill. 'That's disgusting.'

'I'm going to count up to one,' said Bowler. 'And if you're not gone by then . . .'

I walked away with the gob of Bowler on my sweatshirt, like a badge saying: this guy is doomed. For a while I didn't know where I was going; then I got into a hot phone box at the top end of Micklegate, near the Bar, and what I was doing on an instinctive level as I dialled was actually sheltering within the Bar Walls, using them for protection. I called the number that Cooper had given me.

A guy answered; London accent but not Cooper.

'Is Cooper there?'

There was no answer to this question.

'I said, is Cooper there?'

'Which one?'

'Are you his brother?'

No answer for a long time, then: 'I'm thinking about it.'

'But you must know whether you are or not.'

'Yeah,' said the guy, '*I* fucking know. But my problem is you. I don't know whether you're the law or Inland Revenue. Or fucking what.'

'Listen: do you know a guy called Neville?'

No answer for an even longer time, so I had to say: 'Do you fucking *know* him?'

After about half a minute the guy said: 'Not particularly.'

'Well, I'm calling from up north. He's coming up here to waste me.'

'Is your name Flynn?'

'No,' I said, 'that must be some other guy in the north he's coming to waste. How many fucking ones are there?'

'I know you,' said Cooper's brother. 'You're Mr Twenty Grand. Neville needs twenty grand off you.'

'But he's already on his way to sort me out.'

'That's bollocks,' said the guy, who seemed really offended that I didn't know about Neville's arrangements.

'He's not going up there until . . . well, you don't fucking worry about that. Today's, like, the ninth of August, get down here with the money by the *end* of August, and you'll be saving him a long car journey.'

'So what . . . August the thirty-first?'

'Yeah. Look, Nev comes here on Saturdays so bring it on the last Saturday. That's August twenty-eighth.'

'The twenty-eighth,' I said. 'Any particular time?'

'No.'

'If this is serious, I'm just going to take off.'

'Try it,' he said, 'but we've got your address, and we'll just rape your fucking sister, and go on from there.'

'I haven't got a sister.'

'Don't be so fucking pedantic. And listen, you nonce: you go to Old Bill about this and you know what's going to happen, right? You'll be dead.'

'Yeah, but I'm going to be dead anyway, so it's a stupid fucking threat, isn't it?'

'You're not dead yet, are you? You've been given a fucking lifeline.'

'But I haven't *got* twenty grand.'

'Yeah,' said the guy, 'but it's, like, not my problem.'

He took after his fucking brother.

Seven

Even though Lacey was in the Sea Cadets and so on, he wasn't a wimp, just weird and clever. It had been his idea to write Baz Carter's name on the War Memorial – he had a sort of love–hate relationship with York City – and he was definitely into a bit of craziness from time to time, which is where our game of setting each other tasks came in.

A task might be to crawl along the waste pipe that ran under the top of Clifton Bridge, or sniff Tipp-Ex thinners and then just not do or say anything stupid for five minutes, which is not as easy as it sounds; or hold a banger in your hand when it went off; or eat an onion; or swim across Hogg's Pond at night with no clothes on and the weeds shining green in the black water, stroking your dick, and threatening to give you a hard-on.

The first time the cops were involved was when we took Lacey's mother's car. We would've been thirteen. I don't think it was a task as such, just one of my ideas for getting a buzz – which were always that bit more iffy than Lacey's.

It's not hard to drive a car, as long as you can see over the dashboard that is. We started taking it quite slowly around the streets of Lacey's estate with me driving and Lacey squirming on the passenger seat – he had his seat belt on, for God's sake – and saying, 'Keep it below thirty, it's a built-up area', while I was thinking, 'I am the master of this monster', although in fact it was a Nissan Cherry, nothing monstrous about it.

Then I saw his mother in the rear-view, running towards us

and looking ridiculous, like most women when they're trying to run. I gradually increased the speed and the faster I went the more ridiculous she looked. His mother did call the cozzers but when it came to it she refused to give evidence, so it wasn't taken any further. After that, I decided to leave her alone, although it didn't really work out like that.

The incident with the Nissan was followed by my first burglary, which, as I've said, I did with Lacey on his estate. I didn't like Lacey's estate, and nor did he: it was full of roads that didn't lead anywhere except into each other. At least Chantry Row was a proper street, meaning it actually went somewhere.

Nothing was what it *seemed* on Lacey's estate. You'd think you'd come across a dead end but there'd be a little snicket so you could dribble through into the next not quite dead end; and the pub on the estate served meals around the clock and was surrounded by climbing frames and little kiddies' rides . . . so it wasn't really a pub at all. Through the window I used to see the blokes who played darts and watched racing on the telly in the main bar, trying to keep pub traditions going, and I felt sorry for them.

In the middle of the estate was a wood, and they kept shaving bits off it to build more houses. Obviously the builders were itching to chop down the wood, but that would have been killing the goose that laid the golden egg because the estate was called the Woodside Estate, and all the houses were called 'Treetops', 'Forest View' and other nonsensical things like that. They did build a few of the bigger houses right inside this big dark wood, though.

The family that owned the biggest and most isolated house of all drove a Toyota Space Cruiser and, as soon as an evening arrived when this was gone, we broke one of the back windows with a massive plant pot we found in the garden, smashing not only the window but also the plant pot and the glass-topped table that turned out to be in the kitchen and the vase and the box of brand-new wine glasses that turned out to be on top of that.

'We've smashed everything there is to nick,' said Lacey, sticking his head through the window when the explosion was finally over. 'I think we should go.'

But I didn't think so. Whoever owned that house hadn't properly moved in because not all the rooms had carpets, and half the kitchen was wrapped in polythene. The only things worth having were some railway tickets for London, but Lacey said, 'Forget it, man, they've been used.' I didn't know how he could tell.

Then I had the idea of breaking all the other windows in the house. Lacey helped, but basically he was not into it. He spent all his time breaking just one pane of glass, but the way I look at it . . . it doesn't matter how smashed a window is, the question is: is it smashed or not?

Once every window was broken – and that was the first and last time I've trashed a house on a job – Lacey ran off, but I walked, making a point of not going fast, and as I turned the corner of the street a man came out of the woods with a dog on a lead, and watched me go past.

The next day the *New Yorkshire Leader* said: 'A youth was disturbed as he broke into a house in Treetops Close, Woodside. A passer-by challenged the youth, who ran off. He was in his late teens, and wearing a blue and red jacket.'

Not a word of truth in it.

Eight

After making that phone call I was magnetized back towards the little pubs in Leeman Road, which meant going over Clifton Bridge, which meant parking the Palm Beach and looking down.

There's something about trackside that attracts jazz-mag readers, carpet-burners, and weirdos who sit in dented little Fiestas listening to the cops on short-wave radio, etc., but at first there was no one to be seen.

There was still the tower, for watching operations. It looked like the pulpit in a church, hanging at the top of a ladder, with a sort of car headlamp fixed above it. There used to be a shack for the railway blokes, now there was a Portakabin. As I watched, a big, hard-looking bloke with a quiff came out. I'd seen him before – he was wearing an orange jerkin: a 'hi-vis', as Lacey used to call them. Above the door that he came out of was a sign saying ENQUIRIES, but I'd like to've seen what would happen if somebody did go up to that bloke and make an enquiry. He'd fucking lay them out.

As I watched, it was getting dark. The low-level signals were coming on, like half-buried fairy lights in among all the strange railway flowers growing between the tracks. They were mainly purple, and the sky was purple. In the distance was the station: a great glowing hump that I will not use. Behind it was the Minster, lit up like a spaceship. The railway bloke in the hi-vis stopped halfway up the embankment, looking back at his Portakabin, and it was as if something really big was about to happen. But in fact something big had already happened.

63

Just then a train shot under me. A blue and green Sprinter. Lacey would've said something straight away: 'Trans-Pennine', then a number.

I could handle the sight of this train, but still it seemed to make the whole world shake. Not as many go under the bridge as they did five years ago when I hung out trackside with Lacey, but when they do it seems to be more of an event.

I biked over the rest of the bridge, and freewheeled down the path to the little valley of terraces next to the track. The pubs in this area were all named after trains. Any major train that went through York a hundred years ago . . . it left a pub behind. There'd be a painting of the train in question hanging outside the pub, and because there were so many of these boozers, and they were so tightly crammed together, the streets around here looked like outdoor art galleries showing exhibitions of train paintings only.

I walked into one of them. The pub was like an old-fashioned train carriage. It had compartments, and nobody was looking at anybody. There were pictures of trains everywhere, and a big painting of a Sprinter had pride of place behind the bar in the first compartment. I drank three pints of John Smith's Smooth, watching American wrestling on TV, and looking at the grey faces of the blokes around me. The wrestling seemed to be turning the barmaid on. I certainly wasn't. She wasn't exactly classy, but I could see her looking at me, thinking: fucking borstal boy.

I was turning over the options. Maybe I should tell Bill about being in bother with Neville, but there were three things stopping me: (1) I didn't want to look like a wuss; (2) you didn't want to be asking for help with Walter Bowler around; and (3) I didn't want to risk finding out that Bill wouldn't do anything for me.

I was also thinking about Bryan Butteridge. It wasn't as if

his nonsense scheme had gained any extra credibility with me, but I was desperate, and I couldn't get the money out of my head – not the numbers, I mean, but the words, which take longer: *five hundred thousand pounds*. A one-fifth share of that would take you down to London all right: pay off Neville, soak up the atmosphere, stay stoned for about thirty years. That could be the plan. Also, from a more short-term perspective, if I carried on being alive I'd be able to put together a look that I'd been thinking about: Lee jeans, needlecord jacket, suede Pumas. A Supergrass, Gaz Coombes look, old skool 1970s. I don't know what had brought the idea into my head because I don't normally bother about clothes.

By now someone had turned the wrestling up, as if it wasn't loud enough already. I walked out of the main bar, and into a quiet room that had one fat couple in it, a telephone and a telephone book. I looked up the name of Bryan Butteridge.

'*Na then,*' he said, when he picked up.

It was all very quick, unlike with Cooper's brother.

'It's you,' he said.

'Correct.'

'Listen, it's all bollocks about these chairs, isn't it?' I said.

And then something strange happened:

'*So he's toltherin' in't swiddens!*' yelled Butteridge, '*up by Beck 'ole yonder, and he sez, "There's nowt good that's cheap", and that capt owt! Ah were laughin' that 'ard, I 'ad a fair belly-wark on . . . "Gie ovver," ah sez, "ah can't thoil it", and ah'll tell thee summat: ah dursn't soss me yal . . . By gum auld lad, ah'll tell 'ee straight, an' ah ent ratchin': we'll nivver see t'marrer tiv 'im!*'

'What?' I said.

'Someone just walked into the room,' whispered Butteridge. 'They've gone now. Do you ever go to Evensong at York Minster?'

'Very fucking funny.'

'It happens at three thirty every day. Meet me there on Friday.'

I hated the way he said that: 'Meet me there on Friday' – so slowly.

'That's the thirteenth. That's too long to wait,' I said.

'But I need till then. Now don't sit next to me but sit near. Bugger – I'm not going to be alone again in a minute.'

'I don't get you,' I said. 'Listen, if it's all bollocks about the chairs tell me now. I've got no time to waste.'

But Butteridge just shouted: *'Tara, auld lad. Bi good!'*

So I was caught between Neville and Bryan Butteridge: a headcase and a nonsense case.

Nine

Friday the thirteenth was hot, and as soon as I walked into the Minster the sweat went cold on me. The place was filled with a kind of echoing murmur, little bells tinkling, and someone was playing the organ – just jamming from the sound of it. This was all happening in the business end of the church, behind the wooden wall carved with dragons, wriggling devils, and other strange little bug-eyed creatures. I know the name of that wall from school trips: the screen. Men in blue robes were wandering about in front of it. They looked like priests but actually they were just tourist guides of course.

I had my DJ bag on my shoulder. I couldn't see Butteridge, but as soon as I sat down I did see him, three rows ahead, wearing a tracksuit and looking extremely ill. I was just walking towards him when the speaker on the pillar in front of us crackled, and the vicar, talking from out of sight, said: 'O Lord open thou our lips!'

'Believe in God, do you?' whispered Butteridge, looking straight ahead.

'This is a bloody joke,' I said, sitting down two seats away, putting my DJ bag on the next chair.

'I do,' said Butteridge. 'Well, let's put it like this. I *say* I do, which is exactly the same thing. It's useful if people think you've got a spiritual dimension.'

'Can we get on with this,' I said.

Butteridge turned around to look behind him, turned back.

'*Thought for the Day*', Butteridge carried on, getting up off his knees, 'pays surprisingly well.'

'The God slot on radio? Your old man did that, didn't he?'

Butteridge nodded, still not looking at me.

'He used to write them in the pub. He always said he became in touch with the numinous after three pints of Tetley's. The talks were about things that had come to him when he was rambling across the Moors . . . Insights.'

The vicar was talking about fire and dying and shouting, and all kinds of mayhem while Butteridge was looking at his watch. The time, according to my watch, was three forty, and we'd got nowhere. Butteridge kept on looking behind him and turning back. The guy was actually shaking, I noticed.

'I'm going to have to leave before the end of this,' he said.

'Before the end of this fucking *what*?' I said.

'This service,' said Butteridge. 'I'm supposed to be hosting a function, and before that I'm recording a video message.'

I shook my head. I was finding it hard to come to terms with the whole situation.

'. . . In my capacity as Honorary President of the Northallerton Flower Arranging Society.'

'You *do* flower arranging, do you?'

'Me? Couldn't arrange a bloody . . . loan.'

Next to me was a statue of a knight in armour, big Bible in one hand, sword in the other; he'd obviously been a major VIP and yet now . . . he was lying down. As I was looking at this statue I was sitting back with my feet up on the chair in front, doing up the laces on my Air Maxes, still chewing Wrigley's Juicy Fruit.

'Can't you be a bit more reverent?' said Butteridge.

'What do you mean?'

'Take your feet down, and stop chewing the bloody gum.'

'Who do you think you are?' I said. 'And what the hell's going on here anyway?'

Butteridge said, 'Sshhhh!', and started plastering his hair back with both hands. Before – in his house – he'd been calm but he'd also been bladdered. At his feet, I saw, was a sports bag.

'You OK?' I said.

'They've sacked me from my column in the *Yorkshire Echo*.'

'"Cock o' the North",' I said.

Bryan Butteridge *was* the 'Cock o' the North' – it was a famous item that got moved around from paper to paper because nobody read it. Butteridge's old man had written it before him, and to prove he was the cock of the north he'd had a copper cockerel fitted on to his chimney pot.

'They're getting a teenager in to do it. Well, he's thirty-six, to be exact. I've had to invite the little cunt to a party to show there's no hard feelings. *It meks me that fuckin' mad* . . . Youth, you see, everybody wants youth. If the new guy doesn't work out they'll probably ask you to do it. You're a bit bloody literary, aren't you?'

He looked at me for the first time in the Minster, and, with his hair all messed, I saw how incredibly old he was. The choir was singing now – a real dirge.

'Why are we *here*?' I said again, taking my feet off the chair in front.

'What therefore God hath joined together, let not man put asunder,' the vicar was saying, which I thought was something to do with weddings, but nobody was getting married as far as I could see.

'Have you got four people willing to do that job?' said But-teridge.

'Yes,' I said, just to see what would happen next.

Butteridge leant forwards, reached into his bag. He pulled

out an envelope, A4 format, as the invisible vicar was saying: '. . . the resurrection of the body and the life everlasting. Amen.'

'Amen,' said Butteridge, then, 'Here's four grand.'

Still looking ahead, he slipped me the envelope.

'It's all I've got left. The rest's got to come from the Yank, and it will do. I've told him about you, and he's definitely on for it.'

'*What* have you told him about me?'

'I've told him I trust you.'

It was a strange thing to say; I couldn't think of any come-back at all.

'If you're giving me this money,' I said, 'I'm going to keep it and you're not going to get it back. You ought to know that the guys you're getting involved with can turn violent if promises aren't kept.'

'I'm going to go to prison for a long time if all this comes out, right?' said Butteridge.

'I should think so because you're going to be seen as, you know, corrupting youth or whatever. And I bet you've not got a licence for that six-shooter.'

Butteridge nodded once to himself, went into the bag again and came out with a mobile phone in a box.

'Pay as you go,' he said, passing me the box. '*Good luck wi' settin' t'bloody thing up, ahm jiggered if ah can fettle it.* There's thirty pounds' worth of calls on a card in there. Now I'll not deal with anyone but you at any stage, OK? The other three – you sort them out, share out the dosh; I want nothing to do with them. You're all tearaways, are you?'

'Tearaways?' I said, because I'd never heard anyone say that word before.

'Does any one of you run a legitimate business?'

'Yeah,' I said, thinking of Bill.

'That's useful,' said Butteridge.

'We'll have to have a proper talk,' I said, 'and a look-see at this museum place.'

'The Yank won't meet you,' said Butteridge.

'No; I mean *you and me* will have to talk.'

'Fine. But first go and see the place. The address is here.'

He reached into the bag again, and slipped me a book and a pamphlet of some sort. I stashed them immediately in the DJ bag along with the envelope. The vicar had stopped talking by now, and the organist was off on another solo.

'I've not been in here since the old man's funeral,' said Butteridge, who'd calmed down now that he'd handed over the dough. 'That was five years ago, and I'm being forced by the fan club to give a party tonight to mark the bloody anniversary. Even dead, he dominates my life.'

'You didn't like him, did you?'

'You're a bloody genius, you are.'

'Why not?'

'I'm not getting into this now,' said Butteridge, but then he asked me: 'You know what an autodidact is?'

'No,' I said.

'You're probably one yourself, although you've got a bit of a way to go, otherwise you'd know what it meant. My old man was one. Everything he knew – and he knew a *lot* – he taught himself. He had no advantages in life. I did, because he gave them to me, but he wouldn't let me forget that he'd got where he was by himself. Plus, he was a nutter, completely neurotic. We'd go driving in the country in his bloody Triumph Herald convertible, and do you know what?'

'No.'

'I wasn't allowed to talk to him until he was in fourth gear. Ever wondered why he was called Kit?'

'It was his name.'

'His name was Christopher. He called himself Kit because he thought it had more character. Everyone thinks he was the good guy, and I'm the wanker, but in fact, you see . . .'

'What?'

'I got it from him.'

Butteridge was picking up the sports bag, getting to his feet.

'How soon can this be done?' I said.

'Soon. But remember, it's got to be done on a day when the place is open, between the cleaner switching off the alarms, and all the others turning up. When it's closed it's no good because the alarms are on all the time . . . *Ah'll see yer, kidder.*'

And he shuffled off, not looking at all like he did on television.

After he'd gone, I started peeking into the envelope, looking craftily at the wad, which was all in lovely pink fifties and about an inch thick. When I could tear my eyes off the cash, I took a look at the book, which was about furniture, and included quite a lot about Edward Johns. His thing, it turned out, was 'economy of material and structural strength' plus 'the use of lines to produce shape', whatever that was supposed to mean. I didn't like all this art talk.

He was instrumental in moving things on from art nouveau; he was an influence on Charles Rennie Mackintosh and the Dutch de Stijl movement, but who had influenced *him* was not very clear. Maybe no one had, because it was obvious that when it came to making tables and chairs, Edward Johns was a one-off.

In the middle of the book was a black-and-white photograph of Johns standing over a bent piece of wood in a vice. He was wearing a sort of boilersuit with a shirt underneath, so that it looked as if he was wearing two shirts. He was thin with piled-up hair and crazy eyes. The photo was very old and blurry, and the tools on the rack behind Johns had been drawn over, touched up so as to make them stand out; also a black outline had been drawn around Johns's body, but it made him look less like he was really there – like a ghost, somehow.

I read a couple of pages on furniture-making and the Modernists. I was familiar with that term. I knew that it meant radical guys doing things their own way – no frills, but most of it I couldn't really follow, so I moved on to the pamphlet, which was about the museum: Mr Ollernshaw's House.

There was a drawing of a cottage on the front, and on the back a list of dates from June to the end of August, with opening times next to each one. As I read it, I started to sweat. I mean, I could hear the clock ticking on me.

When it *was* open, the museum was open from nine to five but the next weekend would be too soon to do anything – there had to be the look-see first – and the Monday after that, the sixteenth, was out because I was still on licence, and Monday was the day for Chalker.

After that the Museum was closed 'for refurbishment' from Tuesday the seventeenth to Tuesday the twenty-fourth, and the day after *that* it was closed because it was just always closed on fucking Wednesdays. The first time you could get a clear run was Thursday the twenty-sixth for the look-see, Friday the twenty-seventh for the job itself. One day before D-Day with Neville, if all that was really true.

But Butteridge was never going to hand over the money on the day of delivery . . . In fact he was never going to hand over the money at all, that was the bottom line, because the whole job was a total nonsense from beginning to end.

On the other hand, though, I did have four grand in my DJ bag.

I opened the pamphlet.

'Clement Ollernshaw,' I read, 'otherwise known as the Scarborough Gentleman, was a prosperous farmer who lived in the tiny hamlet of Stonehill (now part of the North Yorks Moors National Park) from birth until the age of ninety-nine when he died in his sleep. In that time he left the farm only once: to see a cricket match near Pickering. But it was "rained off". Unbeknown to anyone, Clement Ollernshaw kept a diary detailing every aspect of life on a hill farm in the second half of the nineteenth century. Before his death, he also created a trust establishing his house and all its contents as a museum, for which many thousands of visitors have had reason to be grateful.' And so on and so on. Very boring. There was no mention of the four chairs called Number One, but then there wouldn't be if what Butteridge had said was right.

It was all ifs, and I couldn't really concentrate. Instead, I was thinking: just how mad can a scheme *be* if it starts with a down payment of four grand?

The next thing was to get Bill involved, and I knew exactly where to find him. I stepped out of the Minster, and it was like coming out of the cinema. The whole world looked full of life, and, with all the church bells in the city for some reason ringing and the whole place sounding like a beautiful giant musical box, I set off for the Old Railway Bridge.

Ten

The door of the Old Railway Bridge was open, but a purple curtain was across the door frame. This was to keep the sun out. Summer wasn't allowed into the Old Railway Bridge. It had been barred.

The Old Railway Bridge couldn't really have been called anything else when you think that, for a long time, it actually *was* underneath the old railway bridge on the line going to Whitby, which was pulled up in the sixties. Now the pub had somehow ended up marooned in the corner of a car park, with just two banks of black stone – the remains of the bridge – on either side, which were probably useful in keeping the old boozer propped up.

The Old Railway Bridge was a bit . . . well, squashed, and you had to suspect that the Old Railway Bridge pub had been holding up the old railway *bridge*. Nobody knew which came first. It was a chicken and egg situation. Maybe they built a bridge and thought a pub would fit very nicely under there, but then why would they have built the bridge in the first place except to go over the pub? But then *again*, why didn't they just knock the bloody pub down, because it had always been horrible?

I quite liked it though, and so did Bill. He did a lot of business there, moving around the split brown seats which were all around the walls, as if the place was a ballroom and not a pub. It was a place where anyone who wanted Bill could get hold of him. You might find that you needed a cheap second-hand VCRor DVD player, and you'd speak to Bill and he'd say: 'You'll have it tomorrow. What make?' He prided himself on that.

I walked through the door, into the hot gloom, looking for Bill to persuade him to come in with me on the Butteridge job.

The place was quite full, smelt of disinfectant as usual, except for the bit around the bogs, which smelt of infectant. There were the some kids near the jukebox who should've been outside on their BMXs, and the darts blokes, who all hung around one particular table, the table near the dart-board, which had an ashtray on it that was always filled with pipes. I used to think that all the darts blokes smoked pipes, but I gradually worked out that all the pipes belonged to just one of them. Their dartboard, pinned up on a big square of coconut matting, was like the pub's shrine. All around it were the trophies they'd won as a team with other, smaller trophies for 'man of the match'. There was no sign of Bill but Bowler was leaning against the bar with some barley wines on the go. Dean was talking to Bowler; Bowler wasn't listening.

'So he was, like, a dipper,' Dean was saying, 'worked ver buses. Number twenty-free, Ladbroke Grove to Liverpool Street – quality from end to end; *lot* of moolah riding on vat bus. He just comes up to ver mark – one little touch and ver wallet's in his hand. Ver quickness of vee hand deceives vee eye. He also did stuff wiv a sock full of gravel out Stepney way, but vat was more like, you know, mugging. D'you know what I'm saying?'

Bowler was nodding, absolutely bored shitless – then he saw me.

'What the fuck are you doing here?'

'Where's Bill?'

'I don't believe you've answered my question.'

I had four grand in an A4 envelope in my DJ bag; I wasn't going to take nonsense from Walter Bowler.

'I have answered it,' I said. 'I've answered it implicitly.'

Bowler started eyeballing me. Madge, who owned the Old Railway Bridge, brought him a ham sandwich on a paper plate.

'Ta, Madge,' said Bowler, without taking his eyes off me. Madge went away and came back with two more bottles of barley wine. The tops came off with a kissing noise; Madge said, 'There you go, Walt,' and I thought: maybe I'm the only person who hates this bloke.

'Ta, Madge,' said Bowler again, still staring at me.

Dean, behind Bowler, was nodding to himself over his lager, looking half asleep. The sun had got at both of them, and redness was running riot under Bowler's hair. Every time he moved his head his neck sucked and bulged in a way that you couldn't stop watching.

'*How* many fucking O levels have you got?' Bowler said to me eventually.

'Five,' I said.

We'd been through all this before. I've got five GCSEs: four from Bishy Grammar, and one from YOI, where I retook maths.

'No,' said Bowler, shaking his head. 'No one's got five O levels.'

'Vey do, Walt,' said Dean, leaning forward again. 'I fink vey *do*.'

I'd put my DJ bag down. Bowler picked it up and looked inside.

'Give me that back,' I said, but not actually doing anything about it.

Bowler was ignoring the envelope, which was good, but he had out the book I had on the go, *The Adventures of Sherlock Holmes*, and was reading from the first page: 'To Sherlock Holmes she is always *the* woman,' he read, putting the book back in the bag and dropping the bag on the floor, possibly breaking the mobile.

'That's nothing but hardcore pornography,' he said.

'I've got an idea for a job,' I said.

Bowler had been about to bite into his sandwich, but now he had to put it down.

'What do you mean a fucking job?' he said.

I looked away, because I couldn't stand the sight of him actually, and started watching the budgerigar leaping around in its cage under the optics. Madge had pinned a York City rosette on the bars, and there was a Real Madrid scarf on the top of the cage, which Madge would spread out, completely covering up the budgie whenever it got too excited which, considering the life it lead, was surprisingly often. I hadn't meant to tell Bowler about the job because I didn't want him in. I didn't trust the bloke. But I hadn't been able to resist showing him that I wasn't a nonce.

'A job,' I said. 'A crime.'

'What do you mean, a fucking crime?' said Bowler, biting into his sandwich.

'You know what a crime is, right? Well, one of those, a fucking crime. It's Bryan Butteridge's idea.'

I knew it was the wrong thing to say. Even Dean leant across and said, in his slow way: 'You're having a laugh, aren't you?'

But Walter Bowler didn't react at all except for a look coming across his face like . . . pain; then he stood up, farted, and put his fat arse back on to the bar stool.

'Do you want a drink?' he said, which came as a shock.

He told Madge to put a pint of Smooth in front of me.

'Take it over there,' he said, talking with his mouth full, and pointing to a table next to a blacked-out window. 'You and me are going to have a talk.'

I did what he said; if he hadn't bought me the drink I wouldn't have.

I sat down, waiting for Bowler, thinking about him.

The situation was that he was Bill's right-hand man. He was the lieutenant. Bill had charisma, contacts, and could handle cash, as I've already said. He had six mobile phones at least, and he used these to make sure that the small ads they placed to get rid of the bikes didn't all have the same numbers. Bowler didn't think of things like that – not because he was stupid (he wasn't; he'd been at the Grammar himself), but because he didn't *care*. So Bowler needed Bill, but did Bill need Bowler? As far as I could see, he didn't, and I think this got to Bowler.

Now the first time I was charged with burglary, the evidence was just not really there; the CPS were struggling badly, but what tipped the balance was 'information received'. I was grassed up in other words. It could've been Wilkinson or it could've been Walter Bowler. Personally I think it was Bowler because the jobs I was doing were for Bill, and he knew all about them.

The second time that I was pulled for burglary, Bowler hated the way I turned out to be a hero, because I came under a lot of pressure to say who I was working for, who was the fence, and so on. DI Murgatroyd had me in four times after I was bailed asking me the same questions. He was nice enough about it but it was a drag all the same because my solicitor, Mr Burke, was wanting me to roll over as well.

I could see Burke's way of thinking. If I opened up about Bill some sort of defence would be possible – intimidation, duress, brainwashing or whatever. Oliver Twist and what's-his-name . . . Fagin. Burke would've had a field day. But I did no-comment interviews, so no defence was possible. I pleaded, the CPS solicitor described my behaviour in interview as 'extremely unhelpful', and I got two years in YOI. After sentencing Burke told me that the 'worst-case scenario' had come about, and I just shrugged because, as far as I can see, it pretty much always does.

What I'm really saying is that Bowler looked after number one at all times. By grassing me up, he was putting Bill into the firing line, but Bill didn't seem to ever understand about this. He'd turn a blind eye because this was his best mate that we're talking about.

I looked over to the bar. Evidently Bowler was telling Dean to stay there, then he came across and sat opposite me. I was facing the pub, and Bowler had his back to it.

'I'm going to show you something,' he said, 'and I'm going to tell you why I don't want you around any more.'

He drank some barley wine.

'All right?' he said.

'Just fucking get on with it,' I said.

'Down in London,' Bowler said, 'there's a guy called Neville, and his thing is cocaine.'

Bowler put a wrap on the table.

'You can have that if you want,' he said. 'It's yours.'

I didn't touch it.

'Now Neville', said Bowler, leaving the wrap on the table, 'brings this stuff into the country built into the bodies of three-wheeled cars . . .'

'What else does he do? And why three-wheeled?'

'What?'

'Why does he bring it in in *three-wheeled* cars?'

'That is not relevant.'

'I think it is.'

'Yes, but you don't fucking *know*,' said Bowler, nearly losing it and shouting so loud that the darts blokes were looking over.

'Christ,' he said, shaking his wobbly head; then he carried on, quiet again: 'Neville sends his stuff up to a guy in Leeds called Micklethwaite, who's black.'

'With a name like that he would be.'

'Now Neville is a racist. Down south, you see, they're all fucking racists – they're not enlightened like, say, me. On top of that, he's been getting a lot of grief from this Micklethwaite so he wants a new contact to handle his business in the north, get the stuff knocked out without any hassle, and that's where Bill comes in. Bill and me.'

'And Dean.'

Bowler shook his head, flinging drops of sweat my way.

'Dean is a cousin of Neville's, and Neville has asked Bill, as a personal favour, to look after him for a while, put a few jobs his way, and just generally keep him out of his fucking hair. It is obviously in our interest to do that, given what's going down with Neville.'

I was thinking: Dean could be my way to Neville. I could get him to put in a word. But first I had to know: 'Why does Neville want Dean out of the way?'

'You've talked to Dean, right? Spent some time around him?'

'Yeah.'

'Well then, you know why. That guy is depriving a village of an idiot and Neville is sick to death of him, just like I'm sick to death of you.'

The stripper, Amanda, came around in her underwear, carrying her beer mug. Bowler put his hand on her bottom and put the packet of coke in the beer mug.

'Naughty,' said Amanda, taking it out and dropping it back on the table. I tried to put a quid into her pint pot, but she put her hand over the top.

'It's free for you tonight,' she said, 'seeing as you've been away.'

Amanda was a sexy woman and she had a thing about me; it was quite weird.

'She fancies you,' said Bowler. 'No taste. I've told her you're a little nonce but she's still got the hots for you.'

'Bollocks to this,' I said, and I stood up.

'Sit down,' whispered Bowler, rummaging in his pocket and putting another two wraps on the table; then another two came; then a whole handful.

'This is a present from Neville to me,' said Bowler, 'and what all this charlie is telling you is four things . . .'

'Rocks' by Primal Scream – Amanda's favourite stripping song – was starting up, and the darts blokes had all stopped their game. (I had a theory that Amanda was the real reason they came to the Old Railway Bridge because, let's face it, you can get a dartboard anywhere.)

'We're moving on,' said Bowler, 'and we don't need your distractions. You killed my good friend Cameron Lacey. You read fucking books all the time; you're a nonce and probably a fucking queer and I want you out of this pub now.'

'That's about seven things actually,' I said, 'and Lacey wasn't a mate of yours.'

I started to put the cash on to the table, piling it up alongside the barley wine and my empty pint of Smooth, and Bowler's Regals and the charlie. It was like some mad game of poker, with the notes beating the coke, burying it, and then starting to spill off the table, but I just let them fall and kept piling more on.

Amanda used spinning blue lights on stage, and these were flickering on the money as if they were trying to make it look really exciting, but it already was pretty exciting in my opinion. Bowler gripped his barley wine, and I noticed that big drops of sweat were rolling quickly down the side of his face, dangling on his chin for a second, and splashing on to the notes; they were coming faster and faster as Amanda got more and more undressed, but for once Bowler wasn't staring at her bush. I'd never seen him so freaked out before; the feeling was sweet.

I knew that what I was doing meant that Bowler would have to be one of the four, which I didn't like because he was always likely to lose it on a job, and I didn't trust him, as I've said, but there again I could never've got Bill without him. I was also getting used to the idea that we'd have Dean along, so there'd be no strength in depth. But the thing was to get Bill on board; he'd keep the other two in line.

I kept stacking up the banknotes, Bowler kept staring, and nobody was noticing us because everybody was watching Amanda dancing with no clothes on.

'This is a down payment on the job I was talking about,' I said over the sound of Bobby Gillespie trying to be Mick Jagger, 'I want to see Bill. Where is he?'

Eleven

When a dream starts you don't know how it's going to end even though you're the one who's created it, and that's how it was with me in the days of Lacey.

One of his little weirdnesses, as I've said, was trains. He was a trainspotter, and his idea of a good time was reading railway timetables – I think he had an incredible ability to imagine the journeys with only the departure times to set him off. He read *freight* train timetables too, which I didn't even know existed until he passed one across to me once when we were kicking back in his room listening to compilation tapes and drinking rum and black. On the cover it said: 'Section YA', which meant 'York Area', 'Private and Not for Publication, Working Timetable of Freight Services'. I thumbed through it for a while – like maybe ten seconds. Every page was lists of numbers, and the whole thing looked like a logarithm table except not quite as interesting.

'Boring, isn't it?' said Lacey.

It was, even with three triple Captain Morgans and a pint of Ribena inside you.

'Except', said Lacey, 'that it's not really', and he started telling me all about loose shunting.

Loose shunting – sorting wagons into trains – was the thing that had kept me awake as a little kid: the sound of clanking and faint shouts floating across the city in the night, mingling in with whatever you happened to be dreaming of at the time. Since then the railways around York have been cut back – 'rationalized' is the correct term – and the only new tracks that went down in my lifetime were going into the National Railway Museum, where steam locos are kept much cleaner than they were ever meant to be. Loose shunting had come to an end in this cutting back, and now the freight trains came ready made but they were still moved about while being stored in York on their way to somewhere else, so there was still action in the marshalling yards.

These were between the river and Poppleton Road School (which looked like a sort of old factory), with Clifton Bridge going over the top of them. They were surrounded by fences but the fences weren't high. So we started going to the marshalling yards quite often.

They really were awesome: a total railway world of miles and miles of criss-crossed tracks with wires above mirroring every twist and turn. In between the tracks was ballast – dirty rocks the colour of coal that it was impossible to walk on – and right underneath the bridge was the hollowed-out front end of a Deltic. It looked like a skull, and you had to be down on the tracks to see it.

There usually seemed to be about half-a-dozen men in hi-vis tops working in the marshalling yards; we stayed well away from them. They walked alongside the trundling locos like cowboys leading a horse, and they sometimes walked underneath them – just to get to the other side. They were cool dudes, and their HQ in those days was a little falling-down shack on a windswept cinder patch between the tracks, with a sign on the door that said, AUTHORIZED PERSONNEL ONLY, although that was a joke because there was nothing inside except a pile of old *Daily Mirrors*.

The shack was surrounded by broken coal bunkers from the days of steam, and things that looked like giant wooden cottonreels, and signs stuck in the dirty gravel saying BEWARE OF TRAINS, NO TRESPASSING, MAXIMUM FINE this and that.

The one that sticks in my head, though, is BEWARE OF TRAINS – a very simple warning. No threats. It was as if the person who'd written that sign had said to himself: OK, I'm not going to make a big deal of it; trains are here, so beware of them.

There was one working shunter in the marshalling yards, and Lacey called it 'the yard pilot', which was fine except that it never moved. Well, we knew it was working because we'd go along there and it'd be in a different place from the time before, but we never actually *saw* it move. It had a colour that you couldn't describe, somewhere between grey, green and blue. The back of it was one big hazard sign painted black and yellow, with massive hooks and tubes dangling underneath the rear end – the bollocks of the thing. The front of the shunter looked like a radiator and, on its side, it had a plaque like Bryan Butteridge's house, but we could never make out what the plaque said. From a distance the shunter looked small but, when you got near, it was as big as a house, although what it really reminded me of was an electricity generating station.

The shunter was frightening; the whole marshalling yard was a frightening place – that was what was good about it – and Lacey was into the buzz of going there just as much as I was.

When a train went through, the ground started leaping, and you couldn't talk while it was happening. The trains might be a quarter-mile long and all the trucks exactly the same; the trucks might be shaped like torpedoes with ladders going up the side; I saw one train that was forty yellow cranes in a row.

At nine o'clock on Wednesday, 20 July 1994, when the clouds were a complicated orange pattern mingling in with the vibrating black overhead wires, I saw a parked chain of hopper wagons covered in white dust. On the side of each one of them was written in fading blue paint, 'World Bulk'; just 'World Bulk' over and over again – as if you hadn't got the message after the first one.

'It's one outrageous mother,' said Lacey, as we stood on the little gravel hill alongside it. 'It's obscene. I think it's carrying cement from down south, and it's probably going to be going to the Forth Yard.'

He stopped talking at that point because I'd gone between two of the wheels. I was lying on the track, settling down, and wriggling to get the JPS out of the top pocket of my Levi jacket, and thinking: there's nothing underneath these fucking wagons apart from axles and the oil boxes next to the wheels . . . it's fucking disappointing.

Lacey was crouching down, talking to me through the wall of wheels.

'No, man,' he said. 'You've got to come out of there.'

'Why?' I said, looking at Lacey's trainers moving about too fast, showing how worried he was.

'Because this is serious machinery – it can do you in. Every one of these fucking wheels is a bacon-slicer, man.'

After a while I got bored of being underneath the train, so I crawled out on the opposite side to the one that Lacey was on. I was on the river side of the train, Lacey was on the school side and, even though I didn't say anything, he knew exactly what he had to do. He had to come through the train himself.

I was sitting on the black stones, waiting, looking down at my brown, flat belly (I had nothing on under my jean jacket), and thinking how fucking beautiful I was, because this was pre-brambles. For some reason I looked forwards, towards the front of the 'World Bulk' train.

The shunter was there; its exhaust pipe pointed upwards.

As I watched, one dirty great ball of smoke came out of the exhaust sending little black particles spinning into the air, and then they stopped the clock on me. The next thing was that the train was moving, and I was shouting; and I kept on shouting.

When the shunter had taken the train away, the world felt completely empty, and I was standing looking with half an eye at a sort of package on the tracks – something too small to be a person. A railway man was running fast towards me.

Twelve

Bill, it turned out, had been in the bogs doing coke. Earlier on he'd been sorting out one of his sponsored swims with under-age kids.

Every youngster who worked for Bill started by doing sponsored swims. They were nothing to do with sponsorship or swimming, so the name was a bit misleading. Basically, he got the kids to walk around a certain area of York where their faces were not known, knocking on doors, and saying they were going to do a sponsored swim in aid of whatever. Multiple sclerosis was always a good one. It was all about getting a look in people's houses, and spotting the easy ones to do. The kids had to ask when would be a good time to collect the money and when wouldn't. If a whole sponsored swim turned up only one good possibility for a job then it was worth it. The kids who did it got paid in Es, and the beauty of it was that if the worst came to the worst, and they came under suspicion, they could just actually do the swim and pass the money on to charity.

But it never came to that.

Now Bill was sitting with his feet up watching the pub telly. On one side of Bill was Dean; on the other was Ingrid, who looked very ill and very beautiful even though she'd dyed her hair orange. She was drinking Lucozade – which was the same colour as her hair – and talking to Madge and Amanda, who'd put on a Chinese-looking dressing-gown. Ingrid always came down to the Old Railway Bridge with Bill on Fridays, and it was very interesting to watch her as Amanda stripped: she was the only person in the place with an expression on her face that you couldn't understand.

Bill was reminding of a gypsy – out of time. He wore a white shirt with the top three buttons undone; his hair was pushed back, and his sideburns, I noticed, were growing long. He was watching an evening race meeting on the telly. The camera was high up, looking down on some horses walking around in a circle on incredibly green grass. The sound was turned down.

'All right, Bill?' I said, keen to get started, but Bill's mobile went straightaway. It was always on the cards that this would happen – I mean, Bill had so *many* mobiles. But it really pissed me off.

'Neville!' said Bill.

That fucking name was like a blade – went right into me every time I heard it.

'Nice to hear you, mate.'

'Put him on,' said Bowler, and this was heavy: Bowler's head was really throbbing.

Bill was immediately eyeballing Bowler, and saying into the phone: 'About midday, sounds great. Yeah, that's no trouble to arrange.'

'Put him on,' said Bowler.

'I don't carry a diary, Neville, for obvious reasons. Yeah, that's too right, man . . .'

'Put the fucker *on*,' said Bowler, as Bill kept on talking. Normally I would've quite appreciated this amount of needle going on, but in the present situation I wasn't so sure. I just wanted to keep my own ball rolling, and I needed the personnel, and I needed the *unity*. It didn't come to anything though, because Bill was saying: 'Walter . . . you remember Walter? . . . He wants a word.'

He gave the phone to Bowler, but he hadn't lost face,

because he'd kept Bowler dangling beautifully until the last possible moment. Bowler took the mobile and moved away from the rest of us.

'Nev? Walt,' he said, and his voice was wobbly like his body. Then he froze, with nothing moving on him but sweat. 'I didn't call you a fucker, Nev, I swear.'

'You fucking did,' said Bill, and he was laughing in my direction. Even with all the bother I was in, it made me feel great.

'Shouldn't call Neville a fucker,' said Dean, shaking his head. 'What is ver guy *finking* of?'

Bowler rolled away with the phone, saying sorry over and over again, and he did seem to get the situation sorted after a while because, over near the bar, he got into a long conversation with Neville, and, as he talked, he kept looking up at me and Bill now and again, but especially me.

Bill seemed quite chilled out, though.

I sat down under the TV, right opposite him.

'Can I talk about a little project I've been thinking of, Bill?'

'Better wait until Walter's finished cleaning Neville's bottom with his tongue,' he said.

That was fine; I knew he'd say we had to wait for Bowler.

'You got a bet on, Bill?' I said, pointing up at the telly.

'I've had a Heinz,' said Bill.

'A Heinz?'

'Fifty-seven varieties,' said Bill, lighting a Silkie. 'Fifty-seven bets.'

Dean was leaning forward and nodding at me, showing he was impressed.

'Fifty-seven bets in one race,' he said. 'Vat's a *lot*.'

'It's not fifty-seven bets in one race,' said Bill, scratching his ear and maybe nearly smiling. 'It's fifty-seven bets over six races.'

Bill put down his lighter and his ciggie.

'Look,' he said, and I could see he was enjoying himself, 'if only one horse wins you get nothing. If two win you've got a double up: horse one and horse two. If three win you've got three doubles and one treble: one and two, one and three, two and three, and one, two and three. Four winners, and you've got six doubles up, meaning one and two, one and three, one and four, two and three, two and four and three and four. Plus, you've got four trebles up. So: one, two and three; one, two and four; one, three and four; two, three and four. On top of that you've got an accumulator: one, two, three and four . . . Are you following me?'

'I'm not,' said Dean.

Now Bowler came back, handing the phone to Dean, who took it, said, 'Wotcher, Nev!', listened for a while, then said, 'Aw, pukka! Cheers, mate.' And that was it.

He gave the phone back to Bill.

'Nev's going to sort me out wiv a season ticket for vee 'ammers,' he said, handing the phone back to Bill.

'I'm sure we're all over the fucking moon about that,' said Bowler. 'This joker wants to say something, Bill,' said Bowler, pointing at me.

Bill nodded to himself a few times.

'Go on,' he said.

I told him all about the four chairs called Chair Number One, and showed him the money – all except for a grand which was already in the saggy pocket of Bowler's jogging bottoms.

When I'd finished, Dean was the first to come in.

'I'm up for it,' he said, but I was watching Bill.

'What do you think?' he said to Bowler.

It was useful that Bowler had trousered the grand, because it meant he couldn't actually trash the scheme. But in fact he just seemed to be fucking . . . keen.

'Yeah,' he said. 'Sounds like a nice little set-up.'

It wasn't natural, and then I thought: what's this guy been saying to Neville? And what's Neville been saying to him? Bill leant over to me; I could smell the booze on him but he was a handsome bloke so you didn't mind so much.

'Are you sure Butteridge isn't after your ring?'

'You're saying the guy's gay?'

Dean was nodding.

'Most fucking norverners are puffs,' he said, 'present company excepted.'

Bill sat back, blowing smoke.

'I'd have to talk to him myself,' he said after a while.

'He won't, Bill,' I said. 'He'll only deal with me.'

'No,' said Bill, shaking his head, 'won't have that.'

And he stood up.

'Shall we go and see him, Walt?'

Bowler nodded fast. He didn't normally do that; he was giving me the creeps.

'When are you going to go and see him then, Bill?' I said.

'Now,' said Bill.

'You can't go now,' I said. 'He's having a big do for all his posh media mates.'

'Good,' said Bowler. 'I fancy a bit of a drink but first I want another line. Who's coming?'

And we all went off to the toilets.

Thirteen

Two days after Lacey went under the train, a FOR SALE sign went up outside his mother's house with a smaller sign dangling underneath saying TWO-BED FLAT. Everyone else on that estate didn't need the extra sign because they owned a whole house, and when I saw that pathetic little add-on, I wanted to knock on the door and say sorry to Lacey's mother, but I didn't have the balls to do it.

In Chantry Place at this time, Wilkinson was doing a lot of whispering to officials downstairs, and I was sleeping twenty hours a day because of some tiny tranquillizers that gave me the same nightmare over and over again: Lacey, sitting at the bottom of my bed drinking tea, playing a computer game, or talking to himself in that fast, clever way, always with his back to me. In the dream, I desperately wanted him to be sitting at the end of somebody *else*'s bed but I couldn't say anything, or even move, in case he turned around.

Before, I'd thought about a lot of things; now I only thought about one. I tried to keep my head together by remembering the time at junior school when Lacey had got some dirt in his eye, and ended up having to go to hospital. (I'd never heard of that happening before: most people . . . they get something in their eye, it comes out.) Or the time he took the class rabbit home for a weekend and lost it – it broke out of its maximum-security hutch never to be seen again. Disaster. He also broke his left arm twice when he was eight, and had terrible hay fever. The guy was *doomed*. He was born to be a child, and that was it – he'd *been* a child, and he'd done the thing he was meant to do.

I was headline news in York, and it turned out that everyone at the Grammar had been Lacey's best friend while he was alive, which made it harder for me, as Mr Wood kept saying.

Mr Wood was the Coroner's assistant. As I talked he wrote everything down with a tiny pen, or maybe it was just that his hand was so big (he was a massive ex-cozzer), but whenever I tried to say anything about the actual *thing* he would back off and start asking how long had I known Cameron Lacey, which classes were we together in at school, and so on. Background. I was actually willing to tell Mr Wood that we had been engaged in a piece of nonsense; I personally admitted to being a nonce. He knew that term because he'd been inside plenty of nicks but it didn't seem to register because Mr Wood was a reformed character. It was as if he was determined not to shout at me or give me a good kicking, or do anything at all cozzer-ish.

As Mr Wood talked to me in the house at Chantry Row, Wilkinson gave him the VIP treatment, bringing him cups of tea which he put down on a sort of doily that I had never seen before; and there was one spoon in the sugar bowl, and one for Mr Wood to stir his tea with, making one more spoon than usual. So this was Wilkinson . . . trying to keep his head together in his own way.

I didn't know where Mr Wood's questions were all leading but it turned out that they weren't really leading anywhere, except the Coroner's Court where everything went round in circles. There was no dock in there; you couldn't put your hands up to anything even if you *wanted* – and Lacey's mother never appeared, but just sent a solicitor who looked like Noel Edmonds.

I liked Mr Wood, but he let me down badly by recommending that I see a psychiatrist. This psychiatrist was based in a massive old house with a golden doorknocker. It was next to the Theatre Royal, and I'd walked past many times, wondering who, or what, could be in there, but I could never have guessed that such a big place would be owned by a total nonsense case . . .

The psychiatrist was a woman, and I went to see her on a dark grey day. I was taken into her room before she arrived; the view of the Bar Walls was beautiful, but inside the room was nothing but rubbish. I started reading the papers on her desk, which were photocopied sheets with the title 'Dealing with the Potentially Suicidal Adolescent'. Underneath were headings like 'Wrap her in an embrace of listening', and 'Not seeing her perspective but *being* her perspective'. There were also some notes scribbled on a notepad. Her writing was terrible, so I could only read one of them, and it said: 'The problem of jealousy'.

I picked it up, and took it with me, walking out on my appointment. I threw the piece of paper in the bin in Museum Street, because you can't be jealous of a gricer, for God's sake; you can't be jealous of somebody who's in the Sea Cadets.

I turned around in the street, picked the paper out of the bin – because it was just lying on the top of a lot of other rubbish – and carried on walking. Under Lendal Bridge the river was black and green and smelt of mouldy leaves. A tourist cruiser was approaching, and I could hear the voice of the guide echoing around the arch; I dropped the paper over the edge of the bridge. But that was no good either, because the boat just came sliding out underneath me, and there were all the tourists sitting on the top of the boat, holding umbrellas that were all red, and all looking down at the paper, reading the thing on the water from twenty foot up.

I moved to the steps at the side of the bridge, and ran down them, but they just kept going. Where the hell were you going to end up, if you took those steps, except right at the bottom of the river? It made no sense to me. There were two barges further on down the side of the river, piled with massive chains, and slowly grinding against each other as the tourist cruiser went past. I could walk across them . . . reach down for the paper, but I would be nowhere near. An old lantern, that everybody had forgotten about, was rattling from side to side on a metal spike sticking out of the side of the bridge about two feet above my head in the darkness. I walked back up the stairs, and ran along the bridge. The paper was still floating on top of the water, gleaming in the little bit of light that was left in the day, while another tourist cruiser was coming up to the bridge, with more tourists and more red umbrellas. There was no way of getting the paper back, and the whole world started to go bendy, and everything that I'd tried to keep straight, and separate, and in some kind of good order, dissolved into one blur, with the river and the rain, and me turning backwards and forwards on the bridge and crying, crying, crying, making the whole of York into just . . . water.

Because I had killed Lacey whatever way you looked at it and I had therefore let him down badly; I had also let down Christine, and I had let down my father or, if you like, I had let down *Alias Smith and Jones*, because what does that corny voice say during the opening credits, when the banjo music's playing and they're galloping across the desert with their swag bags full of dollars? '. . . And in all that time they never killed anyone.'

Fourteen

On the way to Butteridge's house I noticed that Dean was wearing the baggiest baggies I'd ever seen. He was actually sweeping the roads with them as he walked.

'Nice phat pants, Dean,' I said, and he said: 'Well, it's Friday night, innit?'

We stopped off at the Big Bar in Micklegate, which plays drum 'n' bass, which I don't like, and where you can't buy a pint of Smooth which I *do*. It was so crowded that you were constantly swirled around to whatever place the crowd wanted you to be. I was talking to Bill and Dean, and watching Bowler as he tried to pick up women. As soon as any girl put a cigarette in her mouth he walked up to her with his lighter, and the end result was that before long no women at all around Walter Bowler were putting cigarettes in their mouths.

'He'd be quite a good cure for smoking, that bloke,' I shouted to Bill, but Bill didn't hear me over the music, which was probably just as well because Bowler was his best mate after all. I wondered whether those women would be more or less interested in sleeping with Bowler if they knew he had all that charlie on him. Actually, they couldn't have been *less* interested.

'Bill,' I shouted, 'how could you handle a hundred grand in cash?'

'You couldn't,' he shouted back. 'I mean, you could set up a taxi firm, call yourself a mini-cab driver, but even then it'd take you ages to process a hundred Gs.' Then he changed the subject: 'When you've had a few lines,' Bill shouted at me, 'you want to keep going with the beers, right?'

'Fucking right!' I shouted, because I was in the mood for a good time myself.

So Bill dragged Bowler out of there.

Five minutes later we were crossing Lendal Bridge. Some rowers were going under in a long boat – all women, all quite gorgeous for some reason. 'Ey up,' said Bowler. Two minutes after that we were walking up Butteridge's garden path, and through the front door. The place was packed – posh York out in force – and just inside the front door was an old lady wearing a long dress holding a tray with drinks on it. There was a queue of people waiting for the drinks and the old lady was saying to each one of them, 'Good evening, how are you?' Bowler was the first one of us to get to her, and she said it to him too, but only *just*. Bowler grabbed one of the drinks, which were full of fruit, and downed it fast, but a moment later a piece of lemon peel came back out of his mouth and plopped back into the glass.

'What's this, a fucking fruit salad?' he said.

'It's Pimm's,' said the old lady.

'I don't like all those bits floating in it,' said Bowler.

'Can I ask your name?' asked the old lady.

'Walter Bowler,' said Walter Bowler, turning to face me. 'This room is fucking crawling with CPS,' he said to Bill. 'I've seen three of the bastards already.'

He went off after Bill, who'd already walked into the middle of the room. He was threatening to spoil my evening, not to mention that old lady's, so I was glad to see the back of him; there was probably going to be bother when he got face to face with Butteridge, but worrying about Walter Bowler was doing my head in. I needed a drink. I was just about to get one when Dean, who I'd forgotten all about again, said:

'I've got a funny feeling about vis room. It's like . . . spooky. Like I've been here before.'

'Maybe that's because you have,' I said.

Dean was nodding.

'In a past life or sumfink . . .'

'We knocked this place off six fucking days ago.'

'*Vat's* ver one,' said Dean, and he drifted off too, maybe because I'd just slagged him. I felt bad about that because Dean Martin was actually a nice guy.

I walked over to a table which was completely crowded with bottles of red wine. Underneath the table were more bottles of red wine in wooden boxes packed with straw, which meant they were *good* bottles of red wine. On the table alongside, it was the same thing all over again except with white wine, and I thought: no wonder Butteridge is broke.

Moving away from the table, but with only a glass of orange juice in his hand . . . I couldn't believe it . . . it was Geoff Boycott. He was wearing a white shirt with the sleeves rolled up to just below the elbows. He looked good, quite cool, and he was talking to a woman who had glasses around her neck on a chain, saying: 'Kit could have played first-class cricket, no question. He was a genuine pace bowler, and he could bat a bit too.'

The woman said something, and then Boycott said: 'Bryan? No. He can't bat and he can't bowl.'

The woman said something else, and Boycott said: 'No. Look, I don't want to talk about him any more.'

But he didn't mind drinking the guy's orange juice, I noticed.

Next to me, a man in a suit was pouring a glass of wine for himself, and the drink came out with a warm, glugging noise: the sound of money and nothing to worry about. I thought: Christ, it's the fucking Lord Mayor, then I thought no . . .

but it could've been. He had the same sticky-out ears.

'Isn't it glorious, though?' he was saying, talking about the wine or the house, or the whole of his life for all I knew – he *was* the Lord Mayor after all. (Or he might've been.)

Looking around the room, I spotted my brief, Andy, who'd done my mitigation at Youth Court when I'd got YOI. Andy was too old to be called Andy but otherwise I'd had no complaints. I thought about moving away but he'd already seen me.

'How was YOI?' he said, not shaking me by the hand, I noticed.

'It was fine. I read a lot.'

'Go to university now, please,' he said, and that was it, he'd moved on.

I *did* want to talk to someone actually, which is unusual for me. As well as that dentist taste, the charlie had given me a burning feeling in my chest as if a cigarette was stuck in there, and I just felt that if someone asked me a question I would give them a very good answer. The trouble was that I was surrounded by the sort of people you see in Betty's café, eating teacakes. I went to Betty's once with Christine; we ordered fish and chips, and the fish came with a slice of lemon inside a silver squeezer because Betty's was a strange kind of place: northern, and yet *not*. These Butteridge people were like that. They had Yorkshire accents but it was as if they were on stage, or just permanently taking the piss.

I picked up a glass of wine, and walked over towards the garden, but on my way I passed Bowler. He was on his own, no sign of Bill, and leaning over a little table, talking on a white phone. Probably, I thought, he won't have asked permission to do that. I could hear him saying: 'I'm surrounded by them up here, Nev. Fucking nonsense cases, I'll tell you . . .'

I carried on walking past quickly because I didn't want to

know any more. All I could do was stick with what I had, which was a very very iffy idea for getting a share of half a million quid; and I didn't want to be near anybody saying words like 'Neville' or 'Nev'.

The first thing I saw in the garden was two old blokes sitting on the patio in wheelchairs – identical twins, both talking hardcore Yorkshire.

'I love the way you say that,' said a posh bird who was crouching in front of the blokes.

They'd been talking but now they'd gone quiet, as if they were a coin-operated amusement and the money had run out.

'Two old shepherds from Egton Moor,' said the posh bird, turning around to me, 'aren't they amazing?'

I thought: why are you telling *me* this?

'These two', she said, pointing to the old blokes in the wheelchairs, who were now asleep, 'were in one of the all-time classic Butteridge programmes.'

'*Rambling*?', I said, 'or *Wayfarin'*?'

'How could anybody confuse the two?' said the posh bird, '*Rambling* is a whimsical, cosy, chocolate-box, theme-park version of the north, whereas *Wayfarin'* was this wonderful combination of being lyrical and hard-edged. As a broadcaster Bryan Butteridge is an absolute joke compared to his father.'

The posh bird was looking over my head.

'You'd better stop talking now,' she said. 'The speeches have started.'

I turned and saw Butteridge leap up out of the crowd on to the grass bank under the apple trees that came just before the garden wall. He turned around to face everyone with an unexpected look on his face: serious. He was wearing white trousers, a blue and white striped shirt with the top few buttons undone and a white silk scarf. Somewhere inside the Minster one bell was ringing, like a kind of countdown, as

102

Butteridge stood on the bank, waiting for quiet. It was still hot, but the sky was turning slightly orange; I could hear wood pigeons making their chugging noise, and the air smelt of new-mown grass mingling with cigarette smoke.

'Well, 'e were the greatest, weren't 'e?' said Butteridge. 'The greatest Yorkshireman of his generation.'

Somebody whooped, and somebody else, who looked sort of like Henry the Eighth, shouted, 'Bar bloody none!'

'Fred Trueman', Butteridge carried on, 'once said that standing next to my dad he felt like a Londoner. He felt like somebody who came from . . . I don't know . . . Leytonstone. And do you know the reason that Kit Butteridge could talk to ordinary Yorkshire folk in their own voices? It was because he was from humble origins himself.

'In his youth, of course, he'd been down the pit. Only for a day, but what a day it was. Hour in, hour out, he toiled away until, at one o'clock, it was finally lunchtime or dinnertime as old Kit always called it. Then came the afternoon which if anything was even longer and more soul-destroying than the morning, but in his back pocket he had his passport to mega-stardom: an offer of a job on the *Hunmanby Gazette*, which is where he started the very next day, and where, over time, he acquired his vast, encyclopaedic knowledge of Hunmanby.

'It wasn't long before old Kit became London correspondent for the *Yorkshire Post*, and it was at this time, bashing away on that big old Imperial typewriter of his, that he produced some of his most memorable expenses claims. He was living high on the hog, breakfasting at Simpson's, dining at the Ritz, and do you know what he called it?'

'Supping with the devil,' said the man standing next to me. Recognizing the bloke's voice, I realized that this was Butteridge's man in London, his agent, and I remembered the name: Darnell.

'He called it supping with the devil,' said Butteridge. 'He couldn't wait to get back up here to the Broad Acres, to watch the cloud shadows sweeping in convoys down the rolling purple valleys of the North York Moors, to see the swarming brown and red fish in crystalline streams as clear as air . . .'

'He does this as well as anyone, you know,' Darnell was saying to another bloke who was standing just behind him.

'Better than his father?' said this second bloke, who looked boggle-eyed because of strong specs, and was shitfaced.

'No, not better than Kit Butteridge,' said Darnell. 'Kit Butteridge, you see, was the greatest professional Yorkshireman that's ever lived.'

'I know,' said the second man, sounding incredibly bored all of a sudden.

'He made all the others look like amateurs,' said Darnell.

Then the drunken bloke asked Darnell: 'You don't know where I could get a refill, do you?'

'Put it like this,' said Darnell, ignoring him. 'Kit Butteridge was one of the few Yorkshire writer–broadcasters capable of publishing a book on the beauty of the Yorkshire Dales not containing a picture of himself standing on some bloody crag with a caption reading "On top of the world and feeling great".'

I noticed that Darnell was looking at me. It was an odd sort of look, almost as if he *had* seen me on that night, less than a week ago, hiding out in that room with Dean.

'I was up in London myself the other day,' Butteridge was saying. 'Is it my imagination or does it get worse? I'll tell you what: that bloody Underground is a disgrace, and do you know what the filthiest and most unreliable line of the lot is called?'

'It's called the Northern Line,' said Allan Darnell, still looking at me, and dabbing his little face with a little folded-up handkerchief.

'It's called the Northern Line,' said Butteridge, 'but there's nothing remotely northern about it!'

Darnell was looking at me again, so I just thought: fuck this, I'll talk.

'You know what he's going to say,' I said.

'Bryan has three speeches,' said Darnell. 'This is one of them. Sorry, the name's Darnell, Allan Darnell, I'm Bryan Butteridge's agent, and this' – he pointed at the shitfaced man – 'is Roger, his accountant.'

'How do,' said Roger, then he fell over.

'What about Roy Hattersley, though?' he said to Darnell as he got up.

'Very, very professional Professional Yorkshireman,' said Darnell, nodding. 'Have you read his book, *A Yorkshire Boyhood*?'

'No,' said Roger. 'What's it about?'

'It's about his boyhood,' said Darnell, 'in Yorkshire.'

On the grass bank, Butteridge was saying: 'So I said: "Well, you can keep your wine bars, and you can keep your bloody . . ."'

'Parkinson?' Roger suddenly said.

'Oh yeah,' said Darnell. 'I've been trying to get him on my books for years. Now *there's* a promising lad.'

'Parkinson?' said Roger again.

Darnell was shaking his head, pointing at some bloke in need of a haircut: 'Simon Armitage, poet . . . Or *him*, he's another up-and-coming talent.'

He was pointing at a pudgy bloke in glasses. He looked as if he was straight out of university, sort of like a wanker.

'That's Gavin Semple, the new "Cock o' the North",' said Darnell. 'He's streetwise, you know, that's the thing. He's going to be bringing the column a harder edge, instead of all that cosy old sloppily written crap about characters living in thatched cottages that his predecessor churned out, and I say that with all due respect to Bryan.'

Darnell drifted off and, because I was stoned, I said to Roger: 'How rich is Bryan Butteridge?'

Roger was staring at me or trying to; he was struggling to get control of his eyes.

'He's in very, very, very deep financial trouble, and you didn't hear that from me. You know Bry pretty well, do you?'

'Yes,' I said.

'*Rambling*'s for the chop, I suppose you know that.'

'I'd heard that,' I said, which was literally true.

'He's trying all sorts of stuff to save it. He's talking about doing it on a bike now, but can you really ramble on a bike? You don't know if he's actually bought the bloody thing yet, do you?'

'What bloody thing?'

'The bike.'

'No.'

'If you should hear that he's bought one, will you for God's sake tell him to keep the receipt?'

'What for?'

'To claim it against tax, of course.'

'I don't even know what that *means*,' I said.

'Right,' said Roger, 'well, don't bust a gut over it. You don't know where I can get a refill, do you?'

At that moment, the clapping started. Butteridge had finished his speech and started drinking wine from the neck of a bottle – you'd think he'd just won a Grand Prix or something. Two women in flowery skirts, looking fifty but acting twenty, were kissing him at the same time; then they both kissed him again for a photographer.

A woman with her hair in pigtails was leaning across to Butteridge. He thought she was after a kiss like all the others, but she moved away when he tried it on. Instead, she started whispering to Butteridge, who was looking up to the top of his house. Then he was coming straight through the crowd towards me.

'You've brought your pals then,' he said.

I didn't know what to say.

'And now they're wrecking the place.'

He had a bottle of beer in his hand now – a bloody big one – and he was moving across the patio towards the back door.

I followed, feeling I'd let the bloke down in some way.

Fifteen

Butteridge was delayed by backslappers on his way to the top of his house, so I was there before him.

In his workroom, the situation was that Walter Bowler was sitting in the main chair – the one that Butteridge had sat in when he'd talked to me; next to him was a big Marks and Spencer's carrier bag that he'd found somewhere, which was filled with Bryan Butteridge's stuff that Bowler had been stealing, including the little beatbox that he kept on his desk.

A lot of things that should have been on the desk were on the floor, including CDs spilled out of their sleeves. Bill was leaning against the windows with his eyes closed, looking as though he'd just finished laughing, and very stoned; Dean was sitting cross-legged on the floor, speaking to Gavin Semple, the 'Cock o' the North', who was also in the room for some strange reason. As I walked in, Bowler leant across and passed a joint to Bill, and Gavin Semple, sounding totally straight, turned to Bowler and said: 'You might put your ash in the ashtray.'

'I might,' Bowler said, 'and I might not. Who the fuck are you anyway?'

'This guy's "Cock o' the North",' said Bill, handing the joint back to Bowler.

'Yeah?' said Bowler. 'Prove it.'

'You want to see my column?' said Semple.

'It's the first time I've heard it called that,' said Bowler.

Now Butteridge came in. He'd swapped his bottle of beer for another bottle of wine, and I was thinking: is there *anybody* at this party who isn't shit-faced?

Butteridge was being followed by pigtail, who was unattractive in the extreme, and saying, 'Look, shall I call the police? Bryan, *focus*, for God's sake.'

'What's this then?' said Butteridge, ignoring the woman. 'The brand new heavies?'

Now where he got that from I do not know.

'Right load of bobby dazzlers,' said Butteridge. He was staring at Walter Bowler (you had to admire Butteridge; he was Superman when he was pissed), who was getting up out of his chair and, instead of losing it and laying into Butteridge, was walking over to Gavin Semple.

'You say you're the "Cock of the North", so let's have a look.'

'What?' said poor old Semple.

'I want to see your fucking todger.'

Bowler just reached out and there it was in his hand. I wouldn't have thought it would be so easy to get hold of it.

Zipping up his fly, Semple just walked very, very quickly out of the room with everyone a bit sort of stunned. When he'd gone, Bill walked over to the door and kicked it shut in the face of pigtail.

'Right,' he said turning around and looking at Butteridge, who was looking in my direction.

'I've said I'll only deal with you,' Butteridge said to me, 'and I'm sticking to that, so you ask the questions, I'll answer them.'

'We can't have this oaf dictating terms,' said Walter Bowler, but Bill wasn't listening.

'Ask him,' said Bill, nodding at Butteridge and speaking to me, 'how he's going to get his hands on half a million pounds cash.'

I looked at Butteridge.

'You heard that?'

109

Butteridge didn't say anything for about half a minute but just stood there looking jittery, sometimes glugging from his wine bottle, reminding me of the guy who sleeps on the bench outside the City Library, and staring straight ahead in between times.

'You're going to have to ask him yourself,' said Bill. He seemed quite cool about it.

'How are you going to get your hands on half a million in cash?' I asked Butteridge.

'The Yank's going to give it to me.'

'The Yank,' said Bill. 'Who's the Yank?'

'Who's the Yank?' I said.

(I wasn't used to being the centre of attention like this; I was quite liking it.)

'Not saying,' said Butteridge.

'That's childish,' said Bill, but he was still smiling.

'How's the *Yank* going to get the money?' I said, using my initiative.

Butteridge nodded once, very fast.

'The payment for table and chairs together will be half a million pounds,' he said. 'That's one hundred thousand for each of us. The initial payment, in cash, will be twenty thousand pounds each.'

Twenty grand, I thought – I like it. Just what I bloody need.

'. . . The Yank is assuming you'll all be able to handle that.'

'It's just about possible,' said Bill, nodding, 'but if this Yank withdraws even a hundred grand in cash from his bank account questions are going to be asked, unless he's a high-rolling gambler or something and does it all the time.'

'I doubt it'll all come out of the one account,' said Butteridge. 'In any case, we're talking about a respectable person.'

'Ask him whether the notes will be consecutively numbered,' said Bill.

'Will the notes be consecutively numbered?' I asked Butteridge.

'They will be or they won't be, according to whatever you want.'

'We don't want them consecutively numbered,' said Bill.

'You heard that?' I said to Butteridge, who was swaying and humming to himself. It was disturbing. After a while he said, in a funny voice: '*Aye.*'

'Now ask him . . . "What about the rest?"' said Bill, who was sitting down on the floor at this point, lighting a Silkie. Butteridge leant forward with a light for him, and Bill grinned.

'Tell him: "Ta,"' Bill said to me.

'Ta,' I said to Butteridge, lighting up my own fag.

As Bill sat down, Bowler started moving about. He couldn't relax when anyone was being friendly with Bill, even half-arsed professional Yorkshiremen such as Bryan Butteridge.

'The rest of the money', said Butteridge, 'is going to have to be transferred very carefully.'

'Too fucking right,' said Bill.

Suddenly Butteridge went full on: '*It's going to 'ave to be shoved around from Switzerland ter t'Seychelles, to Miami and all over t'fucking shop so that no sod from t'Fraud Squad or any other sort o' nosy parker can find out what's goin' on.*'

'We're talking about quite a complicated money-laundering operation,' said Bill.

Butteridge had finished his beer now, and was bending over, putting the bottle on the floor. When he'd finished doing that – when the bottle was on the floor – I expected him to say something, but he just stood there wavering, looking through the window at the Minster. I looked in the same direction, and noticed that the scaffolding on the tower was covered with twinkling little fairy lights that seemed to be hypnotizing Butteridge.

111

'We're talking about quite a complicated money-laundering operation,' I said, to sort of wake him up.

'Yeah,' said Butteridge, looking at the Minster, 'and there's quite a complicated money-laundering guy that can handle it – the Yank's accountant. His name will be given to you with the first instalment of cash.'

'Bollocks to that,' said Bowler. 'I'm only interested in the cash, Bill. The rest is the biggest load of wank I've heard of in years.'

'No,' said Bill, putting Bowler down in that way he sometimes did, which I liked so much, 'that's the only way you can do it – getting a professional involved. I'm getting quite interested in this. Ask him,' he said to me, '"What's the set-up?"'

'The cleaner comes at eight,' said Butteridge, 'she turns the alarms off, the other lot come at nine – so that's your chance. One hour. There are three outhouses at the back of the museum, and the chairs are in the middle one. You'll have to go over a wall to get to it.'

'Do these chairs stack?' Bill asked me.

'Do they stack?' I asked Butteridge.

'Good question. Johns didn't get round to that till later,' said Butteridge, 'so Chair Number Two . . . that stacks, but Chair Number One, no.'

'Now,' Bill said, 'ask if he's got a video recorder.'

I asked; he hadn't.

'A tape recorder?' said Bill.

'Have you got a tape recorder?' I said, and Butteridge pointed at the beatbox in Bowler's carrier bag.

'I used to have one,' he said, 'but now fatso's put it in his carrier bag.'

Bowler shoved his right hand into his disgusting jogging pants and pulled out a semi-automatic pistol; pointed it at

Butteridge and pulled the trigger.

I shouted, 'Wait!'

But nothing happened – no bullets in the gun.

Moving slowly, Butteridge sat down on the edge of his desk, wiping his eyes with the ends of his fingers and looking sweaty; without making any noise, he rolled forwards and threw up some thin orange stuff into the litter bin next to the desk. I was white in the corner, thinking about Lacey, and the difference between life and death, which is basically one second.

Butteridge was trying to spit away the strings of dribbles hanging down from his lips but he couldn't; they were all sticky like spiders' webs. He said to me, with his face red and his eyes surging out of his head, and the sticky strings of puke dangling down: 'I don't want him involved' – meaning Bowler.

'He's *going* to be involved,' said Bill, 'but he's not going to be carrying, and you have my word of honour on that.'

I'd never heard Bill talk like that before, going out on a limb. He turned to Bowler, who'd put the gun back into his pocket.

'Don't do anything like that again, OK?'

'Fair enough,' said Bowler, but he looked pretty fucking pleased with himself.

'Give me the piece,' said Bill, and Bowler handed it over, no problem.

I knew where it had come from: cockney Neville.

'We're going to do our end of this with total professionalism,' said Bill, talking straight to Butteridge now, 'and we're going to expect the same from you. Have you got this money to give us or not?'

'I've not,' said Butteridge, also cutting me out, 'but the Yank has.'

'If you're bullshitting,' said Bill, 'fine – say so now. Nothing's going to happen. We've all had a good laugh.'

'I'm not a bullshitter,' said Butteridge.

'Can I ask a question?' I said.

'Go for it,' said Bill, smiling. 'It's not fucking *school*.'

'I think the thing's going to have to be done on Friday the twenty-seventh of August . . .'

'Oh,' said Bowler, 'Mr fucking scientist . . . You've just picked that date out of a hat.'

'No, I've worked it out.'

I told them how.

'Can you', I said to Butteridge, 'get the money to us on the twenty-seventh?'

'No problem,' said Butteridge. '*Divant bother thissen*. It's Friday the thirteenth now so we're talking about a fortnight. That's plenty of time for the Yank to get the money together, *an 'e wants ter get t'chairs off you sharpish 'cause they're in good nick at t'moment an' 'e dunt want 'em smashed up*. But I deal with him.'

He pointed at me.

'I don't care about that,' said Bill, who was pulling the beatbox out of Bowler's bag.

I pointed at my chin to let Butteridge know that there was still some sick left on his. I thought about passing him a box of tissues that was on the floor, but I thought, no: let those strings dangle, you'll only look like a wuss.

Bill was standing at Butteridge's desk, sticking two bits of Sellotape on to the back of a cassette so that whatever was on it could be recorded over. When he'd finished, he said that I was going to ask the same questions all over again, and Butteridge would be recorded answering them.

'Ask him why he didn't think of that before,' said Butteridge to me, and I thought yeah, that's a very good point, but didn't say anything.

The making of that tape ended in mayhem. Bowler farted and Bill's mobile phone rang at exactly the same time. Bill answered (evidently it was Neville, calling from a noisy London boozer) and told me to turn off the tape recorder just as Dean walked out. Pigtail walked in and Bowler shouted, 'Get out, you witch!' But Bill told Bowler to get out or shut up because he couldn't hear Neville who was fading in and out, and Bowler kept asking to be brought in on what Bill was saying to Neville. Then Bowler asked me to go and get Dean back in because Neville wanted to talk to him. As I listened to Dean telling Neville what a great time he was having up north, I was thinking how sweet it was to hear Bowler being put in his place, but also what a big project Bill must be putting together with Neville for it to be so much more important than half a million pounds, and what it was that Bowler had been talking about earlier with Neville that he didn't want Bill to hear.

I walked downstairs looking for more wine, or beer or charlie; or whatever. I was wasted. I'd been smoking spliff all the way through the session with Butteridge.

I sat down in front of Butteridge's TV, which was showing a video selection of Kit Butteridge's programmes. I possibly went to sleep for a while, and when I woke up the ceiling above me was bouncing up and down, I could hear 'Jive Talking' by the Bee Gees coming through, and the TV was showing a little black-and-white globe spinning around. Because of the Bee Gees, I couldn't hear what was being said, but then the screen went black and the word WAYFARIN' slowly appeared in letters that weren't quite straight, followed by three words, coming up one at a time: 'With . . . Kit . . . Butteridge'. It was like something done in infants' school.

I leant forwards, and turned the volume on to full, so that I could just about hear the programme over the Bee Gees.

'This is Bradford,' said the very grating voice of Kit Butteridge, except that all I could see was rain, with a steam train or just a shadow of a steam train moving in the background. The camera seemed to be shaking; then it moved position. More rain; people moving about in darkness with hats on. 'And *still* it rains,' said Kit Butteridge. A new Bee Gees song was playing now: 'Tragedy', and the dancers had all started pounding at the same time – making one great crump after another. The racket blotted out Kit Butteridge, so I leant up against the set, nearly knocking the thing over, watching film of buses, houses, factories – all in the rain. Kit Butteridge was carrying on talking, now sounding like he was yelling into a megaphone. 'The average daily wage in Bradford is fifteen shillings,' he was barking, 'the average number of occupants of one bedroom is three, the average working day starts at six thirty, the average employee works in the mills, the average life expectancy of the citizens of Bradford is . . .'

Butteridge was talking fast, not making any attempt to be nice. It was weird stuff and I liked it, but pretty soon I got bored and started wandering around the house again. Somehow or other the time had moved around to 4 a.m., and the sun was coming up. The garden was misty, but I could see Walter Bowler standing in a sort of fairy ring of beer cans holding Bill's mobile and saying: 'Fucking nonsensical like you wouldn't believe, man, but it's a neat set-up.'

He clicked off as I got near.

'Why are you telling Neville about the fucking chairs?' I said. 'You're fucking everything up before it's already started, planning some kind of Walter Bowler special stitch-up time. Double-cross.'

I was out of it, as I've said, so I couldn't exactly talk.

While I'd been mumbling and stumbling in this way I

hadn't been looking at Bowler, and when I did look, I saw that he'd put away the mobile, and seemed to be firing an old-fashioned crossbow that he'd got from somewhere towards the roof of the house. I walked out, and saw that he was aiming at the copper cock on the chimney. I staggered in a circle around Bowler, while he looked at me as if I was mad.

'We know where the chairs are,' he said, sliding a bolt into the crossbow, shutting one eye, firing, missing. 'Why do we need Butteridge around?'

'You'd never get rid of them,' I said. 'Butteridge has a buyer.'

'And you believe that?' said Bowler, loading up another bolt.

'Why would he lie about it?'

'Don't get cocky,' said Bowler, and he pointed the cross-bow at me, but I carried on walking, not giving a toss.

Bowler fired and hit the cockerel with a clang.

'Don't say Lacey was a friend of yours,' I said, 'because he fucking well wasn't.'

'You're a total nonce,' said Bowler, shooting again at the cockerel, going back to missing.

I eventually stopped going in the circle I was moving in, which was not easy, and went back into the house. A few minutes later, or maybe an hour later, I was watching Bryan Butteridge doing a running-on-the-spot dance with his arms swinging from side to side, singing his own Yorkshire version of the Bee Gees. His eyes were boggling and he was in a world of his own. The pigtail woman kept trying to get near him – I felt sorry for Butteridge having a woman like that on his case – but had to keep stepping back because Bryan Butteridge had the sort of dancing style that could very easily turn into grievous bodily harm.

Strange things can happen when you mix blow with charlie;

I can't really get straight in my head what happened after Bill's mobile went, but I know that one thing was clear to me at the time: the job was on, and Bowler had something going on that was connected with it, and I didn't know what.

Part Two *Getting Ready for the Job*

Sixteen

In the next twelve days I lost half a stone, no messing. I didn't eat, just smoked spliff in my chair at Chantry Row. We all had our own chairs at Chantry Row – it was like the Three fucking Bears in there – but Maureen's was empty because she was in the Lawn at this time, which is York's loony bin.

I sat watching cricket and trying to read, but not being able to. I couldn't handle any book with a killing in it, and I just don't like any book without killing. I smoked in the house, which was the first time I'd done that. I knew Wilkinson was worried because every day after his tour-guiding he'd go brambling on his Honda Ninety, and every evening when he came home he'd start boiling up jam, making a great sort of fruit fog to wipe out the dope smoke smell.

On Monday the twenty-third of August at 5 p.m., I was in my chair, thinking about those other chairs, about Lacey, and Lacey's old man, about Butteridge, Bill and Bowler and Dean. I was watching various particles swirling about in the sunbeams, and thinking about how, although Wilkinson did housework all the time, he never seemed to be able to keep up. As I read, I blew smoke across to the big dusty sideboard that reminded me of the front of a train – an American train.

I was resting my feet on the record-player, which was as old as Wilkinson himself. Too old. It looked like a small suitcase, and had two buttons: volume and tone. Volume was broken, and tone had never done anything in the first place, but I knew that Wilkinson (Rowntree's redundancy money going to his head) was thinking of upgrading because he'd brought

121

home a catalogue from Tandy and drawn a circle around a little ghettoblaster: 'Get the best out of your music with this
stylish yet powerful mini-system.' In fact, Wilkinson only had
one record, the greatest hits of Kit Butteridge: that guy reading poems, and sort of muttering along to the classical guitar
theme tune of *Wayfarin'*, which was really beautiful actually.
He'd had a hit with it some time in the early seventies. He
was the only guy ever to smoke a pipe on *Top of the Pops*. Kit
was a hero to Wilkinson, because he was really the ultimate
Yorkshire tour guide.

The phone rang. It was Wilkinson's phone, so I usually left
his answering machine to deal with it, but I picked up and
heard . . . maybe the sound of someone lighting a cigarette at
the other end, then the second Cooper said, 'You all right?'

'What do you fucking want?'

'Twenty grand is what I want, well it's Neville that wants it
and you'd better not fucking cheek me again or else we'll put
the price up.'

'Yeah,' I said, 'as if it's down to you.'

'Now the man himself's asked me to give you a call, just to
tell you it's all on, it's all happening . . . it's not a fucking
dream, man. Time's running out.'

'How do you know?'

'Don't be weird.'

'I'm going to do a runner.'

'I wouldn't try that. We've got your fucking address.'

'But if I clear off it won't fucking matter, will it, you fucking idiot?'

'I believe that boy was chopped in half, it was a fucking
shame. Bye bye, Mr Twenty Grand. I'll see you on the
twenty-eighth if you've got the cash.'

Seventeen

Very early on Thursday the twenty-sixth I loaded up my DJ bag with the following items: red liquorice, the Volvo keys that the first Cooper had given me in case I needed another . . . well, another Volvo at short notice; the few grams of coke – can't remember the exact quantity – and the hash I'd bought off Bill with my cut of the money from Butteridge; Rizzlas, fags, lighter, a map of North Yorkshire, a pen, and the museum pamphlet. In the back of the Volvo was the usual stuff plus two blankets to put over the chairs, and a box of food.

And I had Dean Martin smoking on the back seat. Bill had asked me to take him, because there was a game of pass the parcel going with Dean as the parcel, and me next in line. Bill and Bowler were in London on the twenty-sixth, seeing the linchpin of the entire world, cockney Neville; they would be meeting Dean and myself in the afternoon at Bryan But-teridge's little country cottage, which was a mile to the east of the village of Rosedale Abbey, just off the road to Egton. Basically, this cottage was on the other side of Spaunton Moor from the museum. It was about five miles away as the crow flies but, because no road goes straight across Spaunton Moor, roughly nine miles by car.

I didn't mind being on my own with Dean, though, because I wanted to get some facts on Neville from him. Dean was family, and therefore my best way in to Neville – better than Bill, who was a big deal in York but, from the sound of him on the phone, nothing in the eyes of the man himself.

I'm always on a high before a job but that day was something else weather-wise, even at seven in the morning, when we hit the Moors. The hills were purple, gold and black, and as for the sky . . . people say, without really thinking about it, the sky was blue, but this sky was *blue*, with only one cloud, which was long, thin, incredibly clean, and looked like something left behind by a jet plane. I'd been on the Moors before with school trips but that was all about doing six hours of forced marches behind a bloke called Atkinson, a metalwork teacher who'd actually won prizes for rambling. But this was different because I was finally seeing the point of it all. Maybe YOI had something to do with it, because the North Yorks Moors are the exact opposite of being inside.

'It's like Epping Forest,' said Dean, skinning up on the back seat, 'except wivout ver trees.'

He'd spent most of the time since Pickering telling me to read a book called *Villains I Have Known* by Reggie Kray, which he said was the best book ever written.

'You read it yourself, have you?' I said, watching him carefully in the rear-view.

Dean looked out of the window for a while, then he said: 'It's a fucking good book.'

He wasn't so keen on the modern-day London men. He said that his cousin Neville was 'a decent bloke', but this was coming from a guy who'd told me that Walter Bowler was 'a diamond'. The real giveaway was his tone of voice: no enthusiasm there, so all that matiness on the phone had been a front.

Even though he was quite a little stoner and pill-popper himself, Dean didn't like the way that everything in London came back to drugs. To me, drugs are borderline; they fuck people up, but people *want* to get fucked up so it's market forces or whatever. But that didn't matter – Dean had his code, and I had mine. Because of Lacey, I was non-violent like *Alias Smith and Jones*, and Dean was in favour of old-time cockneys because he liked to think that, although he was a no-mark as far as the modern London scene was concerned, he might've been a somebody in the past, and he sort of clung on to that.

'None of vose guys in ver sixties would've harmed a pregnant woman, or an old lady, or an old man,' he told me.

'But what about a woman who *wasn't* pregnant?' I asked him, looking in the rear-view. 'Would they've harmed her?'

Dean thought about this for a while.

'Vey might've,' he admitted, 'depending on who she was.'

I kept on looking at Dean in the rear-view, and he noticed me doing it.

'Check ver freds,' he said.

'It's a hot look,' I said.

Basically, he'd gone mad with his grand. He'd bought a blue G-Shock, Tommy Hilfiger phats, and a Tommy Sports top, which he wore underneath a short-sleeved West Ham shirt. The logos were giving me a headache, and then I thought . . . how does this poor little guy know what all his clothes are saying? He could've been wearing Tommy Cooper gear for all he knew. I'd had a little spree too, buying the Pumas I'd had my eye on, the needlecord jacket and the Lee jeans, so now my Gaz Coombes look was complete, the only problem being that I didn't look anything like Gaz Coombes.

As we drove towards the museum I read out the names of the places because I didn't think Dean should miss out on 'Bog Hall', 'Dyke Hill' and so on, but he was much more interested in the 240.

'It sounds like a fucking bus,' he said.

'That's because it runs on diesel,' I told him.

Dean wanted to know how many miles had been on the clock when I got it (the answer was 93,000), how many miles to the gallon (not many), and whether I'd had it over 100 m.p.h. I hadn't, so heading north across Hutton Ridge on a road so small that it didn't have a name or even a number, I opened her up. The steering wheel was rattling at ninety, and a clank started up for a few seconds that made me think the big end – or *something* big – was about to go, but as we touched a hundred everything calmed down and I went hurtling right up to the little left turn just south of High Blakey Moor in no time.

I slowed down there all right, though – the left turn was steep. Sitting in the Volvo was like being in an elevator going down. The road was no wider than the car, and it was sunk into a sort of ditch. I had the sunroof open, and overhanging branches kept coming in through the hole, clawing at my hair.

We were driving down into Farndale, looking at clumps of houses spread out all over the valley, a patch of light-green trees far to the west of us, a few cars moving about in different parts of the valley, all unaware of each other; a tractor going up a hill straight in front of us (it was at such an incredibly steep angle that I couldn't believe it wasn't being pulled on a rope) . . . and there was this kestrel that kept divebombing the bonnet of the Volvo. It was amazing to think that one pair of eyes could take in so much. I felt proud of the sight of the place.

But Neville could take it all away from me. Of course, I'd taken it all away from Lacey.

'Got any valleys like this in London?' I asked Dean.

'Roding Valley,' he said.

'What's that like?'

'It's a site of outstanding natural beauty.'

'Yeah,' I said, 'I'll fucking bet.'

I turned left at the bottom of the steep road, just before a place called Low Farm. We started rising up again towards the museum, and, two minutes later, there it was: Mr Ollernshaw's House, the side of it.

It was an ordinary-looking house, but with church windows. The road that we were on split in two just before it, one fork going in front of the house, the other behind; and they joined up again later on, so the place was actually in a loop – a little eye-shaped island. I already knew this because Bryan Butteridge had told me, but I wasn't going to take everything he'd said on trust.

Things weren't looking very good, because he'd said that the cleaner turned up at eight, but it was eight o'clock now and there was no sign of life as I drove past. We drove on, and we'd just passed a farm with a caravan parked in front of the farmhouse, and a lot of dogs wandering about, when we saw a woman coming towards us on a bike. Except for the bike she looked like Cat Woman – really beautiful in tight black clothes with long black hair pulled back. You don't expect to see somebody like that riding a bike on the North Yorks Moors first thing in the morning, or at any other time.

When she'd gone past, I watched her arse going away in the rear-view. It was very poignant. But then I realized that she was clattering into the front drive of Mr Ollernshaw's House, so I reversed, did a three-point turn using the caravan farmyard, went back to the museum, and looped the loop twice on the road going around it.

The first time I went past, I saw nothing – Cat Woman and her bike had disappeared – but the second time I saw her running towards the door with one of those flimsy coats on, a cleaner's coat.

'She's the cleaner,' I said.

But Dean couldn't give a toss whether she was the cleaner or not.

'Vat is one gorgeous lady,' he said.

It was now ten past eight, so she was ten minutes late if what Butteridge had said was right; and she did *look* to be late – running like that.

I drove up to the caravan farm again, but this time I carried on past it, and turned right about five minutes later. We were climbing again now and, to prove it, we hit a place with HIGH FARM written on the gate. Now we were at the top of Horn Ridge, so I parked up in a sort of natural lay-by between the road and the heather, and we climbed out of the car. We could see everything below us now: the elevator road going down to Low Farm, the caravan farm and Mr Ollernshaw's House with the three sheds behind it.

The chairs were in the middle one – or so Butteridge had said.

The tractor that had been coming up the hill was going down now, and we could see its arse-end below us, pointing straight up at the sky. A hang-glider was floating over Mr Ollernshaw's House, about two hundred feet above it and about level with us. It didn't look like an aeroplane, but more like a kid pretending to be an aeroplane, going around in circles with arms stretched out. There was no noise at all, and yet somehow there *was* – a low, growing boom coming from somewhere. The sound of silence.

'What I like about vis place', said Dean, dragging on a Marlboro, 'is ver clean air.'

A few minutes later, Dean was just throwing the butt of his ciggie into some dried-out heather when a couple of ramblers rambled up. They were an old-fashioned pair of blokes, dressed in brown, with brown boots, brown faces, brown hair and brown eyes, and they were very bad news, because we didn't want to be seen anywhere in the area of Mr Ollern-shaw's House.

'Bloody glorious, eh?' said the first rambler.

He appeared to be talking to me, so I just pretended that he wasn't there, or that *I* wasn't there, one of the two. But he was stubborn.

'It's absolutely bloody glorious,' the rambler said again. 'Makes you glad to be alive.'

'Bye,' I said.

'I'm sorry?' said the rambler.

'Bye,' I said again, and he got the message.

'Bloody rude,' he said to his mate as he walked away from us. '*Bloody* rude actually.'

I watched them as they tramped off, walking through a gate, opening and closing it behind them, following the Country Code.

A minute later, at 8.37 by Dean's G-Shock, I watched a red car, a Mazda, driving up to Mr Ollernshaw's House. Butteridge had said the rest of the museum people turned up about an hour after the cleaner, so maybe somebody was early; or maybe Butteridge's information was unreliable.

Actually it didn't really matter what time anyone else arrived – we'd seen the window of opportunity, the only trouble being that it wasn't quite the one that Butteridge had mentioned. I could keep coming back and watching the cleaner arrive and writing down the length of time before the next person turned up, but then I would have to put everybody off, and Bill and Bowler wouldn't stand for that; they'd just cancel the job, and I'd be put out of my misery by Neville some time after Saturday.

'If we turn up tomorrow at about twenty past, we should be all right,' I said to Dean.

'You betcha,' he said, and it was quite a relief to be talking to a guy who just agreed with everything you said.

I took a pen and the museum pamphlet out of my trouser pocket, and drew a circle around the next day's date, making a commitment, even though there were still so many details to be checked inside the museum like sightlines, and *were the bloody chairs there or not.*

But the place wasn't open yet.

Eighteen

I told Dean that – to give us a chance of seeing the chairs – we had to wait for the tea garden to fill up. So we killed two and a half hours driving around in the car and listening to the radio, buying coffees at a little burger van parked on the edge of the Hole of Horcomb, and smoking next to a noisy little stream on Egton Moor.

'Dean,' I said, 'do you think Neville is a killer?'

'Why do you want to know vat?' he said, which freaked me out a bit.

'Just interested,' I said.

'I can never talk about vat. I've taken, like, an oaf.'

I felt bad; the Moors were starting to spin and lift off.

'That means he is a killer. I mean, he wouldn't have asked you to keep quiet about nothing.'

Dean finished off his coffee.

'He might've,' said Dean. 'He might've asked me not to let it get about vat he's never wasted anyone.'

'But that's not very likely, is it?'

'No,' said Dean, 'it isn't.'

We both lit up some new cigarettes.

'Dean,' I said, 'Neville lives in East London, right?'

'Course.'

'Near Greenwich?'

'Near enough,' said Dean. 'Roverhive. He's a river-ish bloke. He used to do a lot of jobs going into big river-front houses using a little rowing boat.'

'Sounds like *Wind in the Willows*.'

131

'Yeah. But wiv breaking and entering frown in.'

'Do you know of any other Nevilles apart from the one we're talking about?'

'Nah.'

'If somebody was in a bit of bother with Neville, do you think you might be able to help that guy out?'

'Ver one in bovver?'

'Yes.'

He thought about it – not for long.

'Vee answer is no.'

He seemed pissed off.

'Neville doesn't listen to me; he finks I'm a fucking idiot.'

So that was great – Dean could cut no ice with Neville.

'I can't fucking read, you know,' said Dean.

It shocked me to hear the guy talking like this, but I couldn't let it hang.

'Yeah,' I said, 'but so fucking what, man? You know?'

After a while, I said: 'Does Neville know a guy called Cooper?'

'Vere's two of 'em. Car guys.'

Then, just as my defences were down, I realized we were looking at the single track for the steam train that crossed the Moors. I knew it was a little nonsense-case train, and I thought I'd just brazen it out if it came along, which it soon did.

As the train went past – with kids leaning out of the windows of the green carriages and waving at us – I didn't like the look of the wheels, but I was doing fine until it let out this incredible scream that sliced straight into my brain. 'Cameron Lacey,' I said, and Dean gave me a funny old look.

At eleven fifteen I drove through the front gate of Mr Ollernshaw's House, into a small car park on gravel that had only one space left. We walked through the front door, and were into a stone hallway full of tourists mooching around;

132

there was a little kiosk selling books with introductions by Bryan Butteridge, and an old lady in a green sweatshirt who was sitting, knitting. On the little table in front of her was some money, and some pots of honey.

'Honey From Mr Ollernshaw's House,' said the labels in olde-worlde writing.

'Morning, gentlemen,' she said, putting her knitting down. 'Are you members of the National Trust?'

Dean was nodding.

'Definitely,' he said, 'been in vat for years I have.'

'Do you have your membership cards?'

Before Dean could come out with any more absurdities, I said: 'We've forgotten them. How much is it to get in?'

'Three pounds,' said the lady.

I handed over the money, and pretended to yawn, which is not easy.

'I'm sorry,' I said. 'I had an early start today. How about you?'

I was trying to firm up arrival times without attracting suspicion, but the old lady just smiled, so there was nothing more to be done.

I started walking around the house, because it was important to know the layout. In the hall, inside a glass case was a big book labelled 'Mr Ollernshaw's Diary', and opened at a page dated exactly one hundred years before.

'Jane,' said a suntanned woman next to me, who had sunglasses dangling from the top of her T-shirt, 'check this out.'

She was American. Her friend, who looked the same, came across, and they both started reading the page of the diary. At the top of the page was the date; underneath it Mr Ollernshaw had written 'Raining', and underlined it twice.

'Today', Mr Ollernshaw had scrawled, 'was a rainy day. I

arose, as is usual with me, at 5.30 a.m. I breakfasted, according to my custom, on three rashers of Mr Walker's excellent bacon with eggs, mushrooms and tomatoes. These I followed, post-haste, by toast and marmalade and my customary two cups of strong tea, each being consumed, as ever, whilst thinking of my various sheep. At six thirty sharp I left the house by means of the front door and made my way towards the south field where various tasks awaited me, viz. 1.: looking after the sheep.'

'What a fascinating man he must've been,' said the second American.

I then walked into the room called 'Mr Ollernshaw's Kitchen', noticing that Dean, who'd just lit up a Marlboro Light, was being lead through the front door by the little old lady. Evidently there was a no-smoking policy in force.

The kitchen took up half the back of the house; there was only one window and it was tiny, which was good, because we would be operating at the back. People had a lot more clutter in their kitchens in those days, or at least Mr Ollernshaw did: big stone bottles, coal buckets, mangles, brooms, clothes horses, pots and pans dangling from the ceiling, and all kinds of bloody rubbish everywhere. There were logs in the grate with a little orange light twinkling underneath and a black kettle propped on top.

The second room at the back of the house was another kitchen – the real kitchen, where tea and buns where churned out for the tourists. I walked into it, and an old biddy wearing an apron asked me what I was doing. What I was doing was making sure that the windows in there were tiny as well, but I didn't tell her that.

I walked upstairs, and through a door marked 'Mr Ollernshaw's Bedroom', which seemed to have nothing in it at all but a bed – 'Mr Ollernshaw's Bed' said a little card on the pillow.

But when I turned around to leave, I nearly bashed straight into a dead body sitting in a chair. 'Mr Ollernshaw' said a label around the neck of the dead body, except that it wasn't a dead body; it was a brown waxwork of a bald man with white sideburns like two polecats on his cheeks. It was a bit slapdash, I thought, because there were no laces in his boots.

Mr Ollernshaw's bedroom faced the car park. There were two rooms on the second floor facing the outhouses at the back – Mr Ollernshaw's this, and Mr Ollernshaw's that, I can't remember. The important thing was they had funny little windows with swirly glass in them.

A few minutes later I met up with Dean in the garden, which was basically just gravel like the car park, and surrounded by dry stone walls. At the bottom of this garden were the three outbuildings, some spindly olden-day ploughs, Mr Ollernshaw's collection of knackered bikes, and a lot of other bits of rusty scrap.

The outbuilding on the left was open. Inside were some racks of rusting tools, and a forge with a gigantic, rotting bellows jammed into a hole in the side. There were three anvils of different sizes on display in front of this shed.

The other two outbuildings had massive double doors that were shut and padlocked.

I was taking all this in as we sat down at a little wonky table . . . Because the main thing that happened in the garden was tea; the whole place was really just an excuse to drink tea and eat Yorkshire dainties, those dried-out lumps of mashed-up coconut with the little so-called 'jammy bit' in the middle that you were supposed to be so incredibly grateful for.

About thirty people were sitting down at tables under a shelter that stretched out from the back of the house, with a see-through roof made of corrugated plastic, and one of them was under sentence of death. Me.

Sitting under that roof was like being in a greenhouse: you couldn't quite breathe. The tables at which people were eating were metal, and so were the chairs – metal folding chairs that were completely ordinary. I'd seen the sort many times before, especially in the bandstand of Rowntree's Park. But that was fine, because if Butteridge was right the special chairs would be in storage, only to be brought out when the tea garden was full to capacity which, so far, it unfortunately was not.

Dean sat down on one of the chairs, and, because the ground was gravel, and because he was such a ludicrous individual, he fell over with the chair clamping itself on to his leg like a mantrap. As he stood up again, rubbing his knee, the waitress, who was young and quite attractive but not in the same league of foxiness as the cleaning lady, turned up at our table.

'Dainties, gentlemen?' she said.

'I've fucked my fucking leg,' said Dean, which gave me one of my ideas.

'His chair isn't stable,' I said. 'Can we have another one?'

The waitress started giving me the once over, deciding whether to be a cow or not, so I sort of smiled at her.

'I'll go and ask,' she said.

She went inside the museum, came out again and walked across to the middle outhouse. She unlocked it, went in, and came out holding a Chair Number One – just one Chair Number One, but in the gloomy little shed I could see the other three, all in a circle as if they were holding a meeting. They were actually *there*, which I hadn't really believed they would be.

The waitress carried the chair through the tourists and not one person seemed to clock the weirdness of it. The arms of the chair reminded me of the arms of a person sitting down, with one flat and the other raised, as if the person was saying: stop.

The chair was brought to Dean, who sat on it.

'Fanks,' he said, and, with the waitress standing behind him, he looked across at me and winked.

'Bingo!' said Dean. 'Ver very fing we've been looking for, right?'

As I've often said, Dean was a moron. I gave him the evil eye while I asked the waitress for tea, and he got the message.

'You're right,' he said, when the waitress had gone. 'Me and my mouf.'

When the waitress brought the tea I did the yawn again – maybe slightly better this time.

'Tired?' she said.

'I've been up since six,' I said, and waited.

Nothing.

'How about you?' I said, trying to keep some sort of smile going. (I was glad that I hadn't had any new brambles for a while, because smiles don't work when you've got those.)

'I came in early today,' she said. 'I got here at just after half past eight because we had a Wallies in early.'

'A Wallies?' I said. 'What's that?'

'A Wallace Arnold coach party. Normally I'm not here until nine.'

Dean was actually keeping up, because he said: 'Is a Willy Arnold's, or whatever, coming in tomorrow?'

'No,' she said, looking at Dean's G-Shock, and all the other ludicrous stuff. 'Not tomorrow.'

'Cool,' said Dean, when she'd gone.

After we'd paid for our tea, the waitress came up and carried the chair back to the outhouse, locking the door when she'd finished. We stood there watching her until we realized we shouldn't have been.

'Can I drive it?' said Dean, as we climbed back into the boiling Volvo. I just pretended not to hear him.

I drove out of the gate, heading right, then made a sharper right so that we were on to the road behind the house. It was exceptionally narrow and low; there were dry stone walls on both sides, the one to our right was the one at the back of the museum garden. But it looked different from here: the grass banks were so high that the bottom of *both* walls was level with the top of the car. I parked up roughly midway along the dry stone wall that was at the back of the museum garden, at the exact point where we would be getting out of the car in twenty hours' time, making towards the outbuilding, going for the chairs.

I turned the engine off.

'Scary road,' said Dean, after a while. 'Difficult for a get-away.'

Another little flash of intelligence from the Londoner.

Nineteen

Butteridge's cottage – which had a 'For Sale' sign outside it – was the only house for miles around, but there was a notice on the telegraph pole outside saying, 'This is a Neighbourhood Watch area.'

'Bull*shit*,' I said, pointing it out to Dean; and then I remembered.

At the back of the house was a pile of logs half covered with a blue tarpaulin; to one side of the house was a generator in a shed; to the other side was a green metal box that was the septic tank, and in front was nothing – just a steep drop to Rosedale Abbey village and the tiny stream that had probably once created the valley. The key was where Butteridge had said it would be: under the doormat. So far, he hadn't really got anything wrong – respect was due.

In the first room, which was the main one, the ceiling was painted brown, and the stone walls were painted green, so it reminded me of upside-down trees. The floor was just rag rugs on stone. There was a fireplace big enough to stand up in, and a pile of grey dust and fag ends in the grate. There were two green sofas with black stains on the backs where greasy people's heads had been, and a homemade-looking coffee table with a top made of tiles. In a corner was a biggish wooden sculpture that had holes in it, like that particular type of cheese.

'Look at vat funny fing,' said Dean.

There was a little metal plaque at the bottom of it, which I read out for the benefit of Dean: 'A token of esteem – Henry Moore.'

Henry Moore was a Yorkshire sculptor who'd been mates with old Kit Butteridge. I knew that; Dean didn't.

We had a box of food in the Volvo. I asked Dean to bring it in and walked upstairs, which was like the deck of an old wooden ship. You felt seasick walking on the floor, because it was uneven and you were rising and falling all the time. The bedrooms were all like Mr Ollernshaw's – just beds in them.

The sink in the bathroom was covered in toothpaste stains and there was a tube of ointment in the space where the soap should have been. 'Anusol,' said the label, 'fast, soothing relief from haemorrhoids.' Dean didn't know what he was missing by not being able to read. On the table next to the bed was a paperback book, *2001 A Space Odyssey*, so I went back to one of the beds, and started to read.

The little raggedy curtains in the room were closed but they couldn't keep the sun out, and every so often they'd blow inwards on the breeze, like surrender flags giving in to the heat of the day. It was a very restful environment, and *2001 A Space Odyssey* was my kind of book, by which I mean that it was short and it had a story. It was also Cameron Lacey's kind of book, being a sci-fi classic.

I thought about the time, at junior school, when he'd walked late into a maths lesson. The teacher (a jittery little bloke called Mr May, who was probably a genius) had been asking times-table questions, calling out 'six times six', and then waiting for half an hour while we all put down 'forty-two' or something like that, but when Lacey walked in May just said, 'OK, Cameron', and read out all the questions he'd already asked in about two minutes – one genius to another sort of thing. I asked Lacey about it a few days later, and he couldn't even remember the incident. That's what I really remember – the fact that he'd forgotten. But it's all nonsense really.

It was about 2 p.m. and I'd been reading for half an hour when Dean shouted to me that Bill and Bowler had turned up. It was a pity, because I liked chilling out with Dean – there was no pressure with a guy like that. I ran downstairs and looked out of the kitchen window at the blue Vectra that had brought the two of them from the station.

I said to Dean: 'They shouldn't have got the cab right to the fucking door – they're supposed to be professionals.'

'Right,' said Dean. 'Bit slack vat is.'

I could tell by the way that Bill was carrying a beatbox, by the way that the two of them slammed the doors of the taxi, and by the way they tried to have a laugh with the driver as they paid him that things had gone well for them down south, and that they were out of it. Dean and myself walked into the kitchen, and saw Walter Bowler, who was holding a sports bag and a carrier bag full of food, standing outside the front door, and looking up at what was carved there: 'Erected 1506'.

'That's what it says on the front of Dean's underpants,' he said, and it was noticeable that Dean didn't laugh very much at this. Next, he put down the carrier bag and pointed at the Volvo.

'Fucking hearse,' he said and then, when all his outdoor slagging was complete, he stepped through the door of the cottage, put the carrier bag down on the table, and said: 'It's my breakfast, all right? Nobody touches it.'

Then he went off to stash the sports bag somewhere.

Bill was already in the big room with his beatbox. He turned it on, and I recognized the tune: 'Enter Sandman' by Metallica. They're all right for a metal band, but I wasn't in the mood.

'Rack 'em out, boy!' Bowler shouted, as he walked back into the big room minus the sports bag, and Bill started chopping out lines on the coffee table with a penknife.

I tried to work out whether either of them had found out what Neville had in mind for me. I couldn't see any sign of that. They would've been giving me some funny little looks if they'd known, and I liked to think that Bill would be saying something, giving me some advice, even if it was only: take off.

Bowler sat on the sofa, knees wide, belly surging out between them, and pulled the coffee table towards himself, looking at me.

'Now sit down here and tell us about the set-up, you twat.'

'Ask nicely and I might just fucking do it,' I said.

'Do you know if there's any good pubs around here?' said Bowler to Bill, as I spread my map out on the coffee table.

Some ramblers were walking past the window. We saw just the tops of their heads because to the front of the cottage was a slope as I've said.

'I'm getting a bit fucking sick of all these walkers,' said Bowler, although they were the first ones that had gone by. Then he said: 'Turn this fucking racket off, Bill, and we'll get the set-up sorted.'

But Bill just slowly shook his head at Bowler, so I had to talk over 'Enter Sandman', which is not a record *meant* to be talked over. I explained everything, and Bill started asking me over and over again about the alarms. I told him I was pretty sure that the time between them being switched off by the cleaner and the rest of the staff arriving was long enough.

'But we're going to be doing the job in full view of this cleaner, right?'

I told Bill that with luck she wouldn't see us, that was the phrase I used, 'with luck', and Bill repeated it in a sarcastic way, talking down to me – it must've been the charlie that was turning him into an egomaniac.

When he'd finished asking a lot of other questions that he

should have known the answers to already (because we'd been over it all before) he said: 'Basically we're going on Butteridge's word here, aren't we?'

'Yes, but I've verified what he's said with my own eyes.'

'You've verified it, have you?' said Bowler. 'That's a big word.'

'So you believe him?' said Bill.

'Yes, Bill,' I said. 'I fucking well believe him.'

Bill started to move his mouth in that way that told you he was angry, chewing on nothing.

'Well, I think there's a lot of dodgy aspects,' he said. 'I don't think it would do any harm to go back and have another look-see, make really certain of everything. I mean there's no hurry, is there?'

Yes, I thought, there fucking is.

'Let's just do it,' said Bowler. 'But what I want to know is when do we hand over the goods and get the fucking bread?'

'We meet Butteridge here at midday tomorrow.'

'That's it, is it?' said Bowler. 'Twelve o'clock? And he knows that if he's not here on time with all the cash, he's going to be equalized?'

'I haven't put it in those exact words,' I said.

'Well, fucking *do*,' said Bowler, and he stood up and walked straight out of the cottage.

I saw him a minute later, sitting on a dry stone wall, talking on a mobile and kicking the tops of some yellow flowers with his Cat boots. Some other Metallica track was coming to an end, and I heard Bowler saying, '. . . your representative'. It was strange to hear his voice floating through fresh air and outdoor noises for a change, instead of through the air of a pub; he sounded small and far away even though the wall wasn't more than five yards from the cottage.

Bill was looking at Bowler through the little bent window as well.

'Got his own phone now,' he said.

'Who do you think he's talking to?' I said.

'Who do you think?' said Bill.

'Yeah,' said Dean, 'who do you fink? Our Neville.'

'What do you think he's *saying* to him?' I said.

Bill had a whisky bottle now – White Horse – and was pouring drinks for the three of us.

'Probably "thanks for having us", that kind of thing. Walter's insecure, that's all it is. Probably does too much charlie – well, he definitely does too much charlie, no question about that.'

'He's making *me* feel pretty fucking insecure as well,' I said.

Bill drank one whisky, filled his glass again.

'Why is Bowler always talking to Neville on the phone?' I said.

'Cool it,' said Bill again.

'He's not thinking of getting Neville up here, is he? To rip off the fucking job.'

Bill's mouth was moving. What I was coming out with meant I was disrespecting him but I couldn't help it.

'Neville's coming up here, yeah. He's got something on, and he's not saying what, but it's nothing to do with any fucking chairs. He's not into furniture removals.'

'I just don't want to get stitched up, that's all.'

'You're saying ver guy's a bubbler?'

That was Dean; I didn't know what the fucking hell he was talking about.

Bill nodded to himself for a little while, and we all looked out of the window at Bowler. A sheep had walked up to where he was sitting, and was looking up at him; Bowler had made his hand into a pistol, which he pointed down at the sheep's head shouting, 'Bang!' The sheep did not know what to make of this.

'Any chance of getting some food together?' said Bill.

'Ver cooker's knackered,' said Dean. 'I tried it.'

'It's not,' I said. 'I've just got to switch on the generator, I think, but I'd better call Butteridge about that.'

'Ver generator?' said Dean. 'You mean vat fing?'

He was pointing through one of the windows.

'No,' I said, 'that's the septic tank.'

'What's vat for ven?' said Dean.

I looked at Bill, and there was a nice little twinkle there. He was a different guy when Bowler wasn't around.

'Effluent,' Bill said.

'Affluent?' said Dean. 'You mean like, all our piss and shit goes into vat box?'

'That's it,' said Bill.

Dean thought about this for quite a while.

'Vat's evidence,' he said.

'So you think someone's going to empty that out and wade through an ocean of shite in the hope of getting some DNA off one of your turds?' I said.

'All it takes', said Dean, 'is one dedicated copper.'

I looked at Bill; he was shaking his head, but he wouldn't openly take the piss out of Dean, and that was the difference between him and Bowler. Bill had a bit of humanity about him.

'Bill,' I said, 'what does Neville *look* like?'

Bill went wide-eyed.

'You sound nervous when you say vat,' said Dean, 'but Neville's got noffing against you. He doesn't even know you.'

I gave Dean the eye, trying to work out if there was anything behind this, but what I got back was just the usual . . . one-dimensional.

Bill stood up, and I went upstairs to lie down on my bed and call Butteridge on the mobile.

''Ow do,' he said, when he answered.

He was *on*; he sounded happy.

'We're at the cottage,' I said.

'Good,' he said, *'Now it's bin there for nigh on five 'undred years so don't fuckin' wreck it.'*

'How do I turn on the generator?'

He explained, and then I told him we'd checked out the museum, and that he'd been basically right about everything.

'Don't sound so surprised,' he said.

Butteridge told me he'd arranged to meet the Yank at a hotel near York – he wouldn't tell me which one – at 7 p.m. that evening, and the cash would be given to him then, as well as the contact number of the money man. He also said he'd already handed over the table.

'Hang on,' I said. 'Who to?'

'To a bloke who works fer t'Yank.'

'So this guy's got a van, has he?'

'Course he has,' said Butteridge. 'How else are you going to move a big bloody table like that? Now listen, there's been a slight change of plan for tomorrow. We meet at one o'clock, all right? Not twelve.'

'Why?'

'I've told you: change of plan.'

'You'd better have this money when we turn up with the goods,' I said. 'Otherwise there's going to be two of us on the spot.'

'What are you talking about?'

'You're going to be equalized. I can't put it any fucking plainer than that.'

Butteridge just sighed, then he said, 'Listen, I've written two possible intros for a feature I'm doing for the *Danby Observer*, and I'm looking for a bit of feedback. I want you to tell me which is best. Here's the first one: "Talk to old Tom

Murgatroyd, shepherd of this parish . . .'"

'Fuck *right* off,' I said.

'" . . . shepherd of this parish for nigh on fifty years, about this Yorkshire independence malarkey, and you'll earn yourself a deal of straight talking. Tom's trenchant views are in line with my own on this one, the point being that Yorkshire is *already* out on its own, because when the Almighty created the broad acres, he broke the bloody mould. Tom knows that – he's spent his whole working life in the finest landscape England has to offer.'"

'Is that it?'

'That's version one. Now here's version two: "Trenchant is not the word for shepherd Tom Murgatroyd's views on the burning issue of independence for Yorkshire. He simply says, with all the accumulated wisdom of the true country-loving Tyke, 'Don't talk bloody daft.'" That's it. Now I'm looking to you as a literary man . . . which is best?'

'If you mean which is the crappest, it's very hard to say. Why don't you just put, "Tom what's-his-name has an opinion on Yorkshire independence: he's against it." Keep it fucking simple for once.'

There was a long silence, except for Butteridge breathing into the phone.

'I've just written that down,' he said after a while. 'It looks quite good.'

'I think this mobile phone's going,' I said, because Butteridge was beginning to sound woozy.

'No,' said Butteridge, 'it's just a very weak signal on the Moors, which reminds me, I've got a new idea for a TV series that's going to be the start of my relaunch after I've got this dough in the bank. Every edition would start with me trying to make a call on my mobile and not getting through.'

'Yeah,' I said. 'Very gripping.'

' . . . because I'm going to be profiling all those places where you can't use your mobile. It's going to be called *No Signal*, and the first one I might do from the Cheddar Gorge.'

'But the Cheddar Gorge is not in Yorkshire.'

'Shocked yer, eh?' said Butteridge. 'That's 'cause ah'm branchin' out, kid. *I've got ter go now any road – I'm watchin' meself on t'telly.*'

'What channel?' I said.

'BBC2,' said Butteridge. 'It's a repeat of an old edition of *Rambling*. They're showing it because one of their transmitters is down, or something. It's not one of the best actually, but then I am my own worst critic.'

'I might have a look at it.'

'Actually,' said Butteridge, 'thinking about it, David Heaton who writes for *The Times* is my own worst critic. You should've seen the pasting he gave to my autobiography, *Yorkshire Born*.'

Butteridge was breaking up.

'"Yorkshire Bore", indeed,' he said, and then he was gone.

I started up the generator, which made a noise like a North Sea ferry only a bit louder, and when I came back into the house Dean was standing in the kitchen with the kettle boiling, the fridge humming, all the rings on the cooker burning, the radio playing, and the plate in the microwave turning around.

'Hey!' he said. 'Nice one.'

Dean started to fry some sausages, but he was a very slow sort of cook, and Bill and Bowler couldn't wait. They went off to find a pub.

After the sausages, which Dean had very slowly burnt, the two of us kicked back with a couple of cans of Smooth and a smoke in the living room, but then I remembered that Butteridge was on the TV, so I switched on. What we saw was Butteridge talking to a man with no real mouth or teeth in a room with flat caps on shelves all around the walls.

'I think I'm going to invest in one of your flat caps, Stan,' Butteridge was saying, 'but what size do you think I am?'

'Well, you've got a big head so I'd say large,' said the man, and they both started laughing, the old man for real, Butteridge only pretending. While they both laughed, the mouth-organ music that was the signature tune of *Rambling* faded in, and the credits came up. It was incredible how often the words Bryan Butteridge appeared in them: *Rambling with Bryan Butteridge* was 'based on an idea by Bryan Butteridge', was 'written and presented by Bryan Butteridge' ('with additional material by Bryan Butteridge') and was made by 'B.B. TV in association with Bryan Butteridge' sort of thing.

After the programme finished, though, a picture of Jed Thorpe looking shagged out appeared on the screen.

'And there's more from Yorkshire next Friday at 11 p.m.,' said the voiceover man, 'when Jed Thorpe presents the first edition of a new series, *Hard*, live from the Get Yer Knob Out Club in Leeds. He'll be looking at the booming fashion and club scene across the north and playing some really bangin' tunes.'

The announcer's voice didn't suit the words he had to say; it was a sleepy, sunny afternoon, and he had a sleepy, sunny afternoon sort of voice.

'What do you fink of vat guy?' said Dean, as I turned the telly off.

'Thorpe?'

'No. Butteridge.'

'Well, you know, he makes money out of talking about the place you live in . . . and he makes it into a cliché.'

'Vat's exactly it, mate,' said Dean. 'It's like all vose geezers who go poncing about saying what a fantastic place, like, Stratford East London is.'

'Who?' I said.

'Telling you something you already know. It pisses me off.'

'But who says Stratford is a fantastic place?'

'Who *doesn't* say it, vat's ver question.'

Getting to my feet I could see, through the front windows of the cottage, a patch of sunlight moving across forests, green fields, black heather, over dry stone walls, like a searchlight being worked by God.

'After London,' said Dean, who was also looking out of the window from his chair, 'vis is my favourite place.'

'What other places have you been apart from London and here, Dean?' I said.

'None,' said Dean.

Part Three *The Job*

Twenty

I had a dream about Cameron Lacey. He kept cropping up in London, and he was perfectly OK, except that he had to keep selling bits of himself to the butcher's.

Then, when I woke up on the morning of the job, the whole cottage was full of a seething sound. At first I thought it was the sound of frying, and there *was* frying going on in the kitchen, but this was a bigger noise, and I knew it meant trouble. When I opened the little ragged curtains at the windows at the end of my bed, no light came in. It was raining, Rosedale looked like a black-and-white film, with more black than white, and a slow rumble came rolling towards the house from across the valley.

'Funder,' said Dean Martin, walking back into the bed-room with the sound of the bog flushing behind him. He was wearing a pair of running shorts and a new shirt. It was still a West Ham shirt obviously, but this one listed all the trophies they'd ever won, which wasn't many.

'My old mum said it always rains up norf,' he said, while I read the list of West Ham trophies. Most of them had been won in the fucking nineteenth century.

'This is the first time it's rained since you've been here,' I reminded Dean, but he was never too bothered about facts.

'Ver job's off, right?' he said.

'I don't see why,' I said, crouching on the little bed in my boxers, looking out of the window. 'This rain is good because it cuts down visibility.'

'You mean we won't be able to see where we're going?' said Dean.

'No,' I said, getting into my Lee jeans. 'That would not be good. I mean that other people wouldn't be able to see *us* so easily.'

Five minutes later we were all in the kitchen having breakfast. Basically, I had Ricicles and cocaine and tea, Dean had Cheerios and speed, and Bill just had cocaine and black coffee, while Walter Bowler went into a sort of trance as he cleaned up egg, bacon, sausages, beans, fried bread and so on, doing what he had to do in order to be Walter Bowler for the rest of the day. Occasionally he'd rock back and fart, then he'd swoop down on the food again.

Bill was leaning against the cooker, not saying very much – 'It's raining, what are we going to do?' is what it amounted to. A lot of my respect for him was ebbing away.

'I think we should still go for it,' I said.

There was just the quick clicking of Bowler's knife and fork for a while, the sound of the rain, and the sound of some really extra *big* raindrops plopping down from the roof of the house on to the windowsills.

Then Bill said: 'OK.'

'Nobody's carrying, are they?' I said to Bill, meaning 'Walter Bowler's not carrying, is he?'

I sounded like a wuss, but that was the price I had to pay.

Bill gave me the eye for a while, then shook his head.

'You've got your freezing agent?' I said to Bowler, and he nodded, jabbing at a bit of something stuck in his teeth. I noticed the sports bag next to his feet.

Bowler looked at me, looking at it.

'Don't stare at my fucking bag,' he said. 'It's fucking rude.'

When he'd finished his breakfast, he rubbed his hands together and called out, 'Nosebag!' and Bill, smiling what I thought was a bloody silly smile, chopped out some lines for him.

154

Half an hour later, at twenty to eight, we were in the Volvo driving down towards Rosedale Abbey, the grey village coming and going between the swiping of the wipers. Every one of us was soaked to the skin because we'd walked across from the house to the Volvo: ten paces.

I had on the bobble hat, and Dean was wearing a sky-blue waterproof with 'Maine' written on the back. The hood was up, but it was so wet that you could see Dean's hair through the top, like a lot of mashed-up spiders. Bowler's face was shiny with rainwater, and his hair was so flat and thin after the rain that it looked like Biro scribble on his Spacehopper head. He was wearing a Ralph Lauren polo shirt that he'd bought with his grand – it was meant to be purple but the rain had made it black.

Only Bill looked good. Even after being in the rain, his hair was springy like the heather on the moors, and the raindrops rested in it like bits of broken glass. He was wearing a tweed jacket and a thin orange roll-necked jumper that would have looked like a joke on anyone else.

Walter Bowler's freezing agent was in the back, and the sports bag was in there too – Bill wouldn't leave it in the cottage. I knew what was in it, even though I wasn't supposed to: probably about half a ton of charlie.

We were coming up to Rosedale Head . . .

'That's right,' said Bowler, as I approached the little junction, 'nice and slow.'

I could never resist coming back at him, so I said: 'There's a procedure for approaching any junction. Check your mirror, signal, then make the turn. Mirror, signal, manoeuvre.'

'Bollocks,' said Bowler.

'Ever heard of Bobby Silver?' said Dean.

'Oh Christ, not again,' said Bowler, and I caught Dean's expression in the rear-view. He was frowning, and then, very

155

slowly (because it was quite a mouthful for him), Dean said: 'I don't fink vat Neville would like to hear vat you've been disrespecting me like vat.'

The Volvo's indicator was ticking. It was very loud.

'Walter's out of order, Dean,' said Bill after a while. 'Tell us about Bobby Silver.'

But Dean said nothing.

I drove past a tractor that was moving in its own rainstorm.

'Bobby Silver', Dean said, after about three minutes, 'was a shit-hot racing driver in his day – Formula Free – and do you know what his procedure was when he approached a junction?'

There was no sound except the wipers and the rain.

'Put your foot down,' said Dean. 'Where most people slowed down Bobby Silver speeded up, and vat was ver whole secret of his success.'

'He's lucky not to be dead,' I said.

'He's not dead,' said Dean, 'but he *is* in Parkhurst.'

'The next best thing, then,' I said.

We came up behind some sheep in the road. They wobbled off on to the verges but took their time about it.

'Bobby Silver', Dean was carrying on saying, 'married his prison visitor, who was a local girl from a place called Cows. I mean . . . can you fucking believe vat? Fucking *Cows*?'

'It's spelt differently,' I said.

'*Shut* it,' said Bowler.

'The place on the Isle of Wight has got an "e" in it,' I said, before craftily bending a bit of liquorice into my mouth so that even Bill, who was sitting in the passenger seat, couldn't see what I was doing. We were coming up to the elevator road, and I was starting to get a bit jumpy.

I turned right at the sign pointing to Church Houses (because I was approaching it from the north this time; with Dean I'd been coming at it from the south). I started heading for the Low Farm turn-off, going down the elevator again. I saw a sign saying '20%', which I hadn't noticed before, then a second one saying 'One in three', which is maybe another way of saying the same thing. Just in case you hadn't quite got the message, another sign said: 'Unsuitable for commercial vehicles.'

To my right was a gate with hundreds of raindrops trembling on it. The clouds above the Rudland Ridge were doing something very odd and unnatural: swirling and somersaulting between the ground and the air – I'd never seen weather behaving like that before.

I turned left at the Low Farm, on to the rocky road, and there was Mr Ollernshaw's House, with the clouds moving fast above it like steam. The second stick of liquorice went in and Bill gave me a funny old look but didn't say anything. I took the fork to the right and started going along the road behind Mr Ollernshaw's House, parking the 240 midway along the back wall, and accidentally turning the ignition completely off, making the wipers stop and the world go blurred. I switched them back on. It was twenty-five past eight. The rain had made us late.

The four doors opened, we all climbed out, and we might as well have just leapt straight into a river. Dean was the first one up the greasy stone wall, and I've a snapshot in my mind of him crouching on the sharp stones at the top like a bird, waiting for everyone else to join him. I'd thought that Bowler would have a problem, being so fat, but he just seemed to float to the top like Humpty Dumpty in reverse.

For a second all four of us were sitting on top of that not-very-dry dry stone wall looking across the courtyard into the back of the house. I thought for a moment that I could see a shadowy person moving about inside – the beautiful Cat Lady cleaner – but that wouldn't matter if we were quick, and we definitely were.

I could see the freezing agent bulging in Bowler's jogging pants.

'Fuck that,' I said, pointing to it as we all leapt down from the wall together. 'Just get the fucking anvil.'

Bowler did what he was told because, although he was a bastard, he was a good thief. It was the smallest of the three anvils in the yard that he grabbed, but it was still impressive to see it fly. It burst right through the double doors of the outhouse, and there were the four chairs called Number One, waiting in line and ready for their getaway, while the rain blew in through the hole that Bowler had made. Bill and Bowler didn't waste any time saying how weird-looking the chairs were – after everything I'd told them they were ready for it. I waited for the alarm; it didn't come. I looked at the back of the house. No movement at the windows, so we closed in on the chairs.

We took one chair apiece to the bottom of the wall and, without anybody needing to be told, made a human chain between the bottom of the wall inside the yard (where I was standing), the top of the wall (Dean), the bottom of the wall outside the courtyard (Bill or Bowler, I couldn't see), and the 240 (Bowler or Bill). We were all totally *on* it.

When I'd lifted the last of the four chairs up to Dean, I climbed on to the top of the wall and looked back at the house. Nothing was happening in there. I leapt the six feet off the wall, landing right next to Bill.

'Nice one,' he said, and I liked him all over again.

Then I turned to the right, and saw the black and blue clouds on Farndale Moor moving in a certain way . . . there was a car in there; the clouds came down again, and the car was gone. But I saw it a second later, snaking down a hill; it would be bumper to bumper with the Volvo in two minutes. It was nearly half past eight.

The chairs were lying about at all angles in the nettles and ferns on the grass bank at the bottom of the wall. We'd misjudged slightly, so the Volvo was ten feet away from us. Dean was in the driving seat.

'I'll back up,' he shouted.

'There's a fucking car coming,' I said to Bill.

'I've already clocked it,' he said.

Bowler was standing there with a massive grin on his face.

'What the fuck's going on?' I shouted.

The Volvo jerked backwards, stopping just in front of the chairs. I lifted the back and we started loading up.

'What's that fucking car doing, Walter?' I said.

'OK?' yelled Dean from the Volvo.

'I'm putting the fucking blanket on,' I called out to Dean.

I heard a sort of half-shout from Dean, then the Volvo started skidding, just standing there screaming in the rain, for what seemed like a long time, and I was screaming too, because I knew what was going on.

The Volvo took off – forwards, going to the end of the little lane, swinging from verge to verge, with the back still up but the chairs still in, and they didn't even fall out when Dean fucked up a handbrake turn at the end of the narrow road, and banged the Volvo into the dry stone walls on both sides. Bill had the semi-auto in his hand. He was aiming at the scrambling Volvo, and Bowler was shouting, 'Fucking do it!'

The Volvo was going past the front of the museum now, fading away; Bowler was shouting, 'Bastard! Bastard! Bastard, Bastard!'

Bill was still holding his pistol out, in a daze, and then, when Bowler stopped shouting, I could hear for the first time the little swirling river that was running down both sides of the road.

Looking sad, Bill put the semi-automatic back in his jacket pocket.

'Why didn't you just fucking equalize him?' said Bowler, who was nearly crying.

'Because he's Neville's cousin,' said Bill, screwing up his eyes to keep out the flying rain, then opening them again, wide. 'And anyway's there's a car coming.'

The car pulled up. It was a muddy red Merc, and there was an old man inside it – a farmer-type in tangled-up tweeds.

'Do you lads want a lift?' he said; he had quite a strong Yorkshire accent.

'Thanks,' said Bill, looking cool immediately, with his hands in his pockets in the rain. 'Where you off to?'

'Whitby,' said the man and, even though I was already dead, I climbed in with the other two.

As the old guy drove, nobody said anything. I had twenty-four hours to get twenty grand to Neville in London, and the goods were gone; but there again Butteridge probably wouldn't have been able to put his hands on the dough even if we'd got them, so Dean had probably saved *his* life anyway.

On the way to Whitby, no one spoke. We were just pulling past 'Whitby Welcomes Careful Drivers' when the old guy finally talked: 'Your mate left you behind,' he said.

'That's right,' said Bill, after a while.

'Why did he do that, then?'

'Well, he's . . . you know, a bastard,' said Bill.

The old man, carefully driving into Whitby, did not look very convinced, until Bill said: 'He's from London.'

'I *see*,' said the old man, nodding his head. 'There you go then.'

Twenty-One

When we got to Whitby the sun was out, and the world had gone back to colour. The old man dropped us off in the car park next to the Abbey, which is a black skeleton of a massive church – all that's left is an arch, and three stone rockets pointing up into the sky. The car park, the Abbey, and a church and a graveyard are on a cliff looking over the town. We all walked towards the edge of the cliff, with the warm breeze constantly fluttering the filthy hair on our filthy heads, but when Bill lit up all that happened was that a couple of sparks spun away as he raised the Silk Cut for his first drag. Only he could have done that.

I looked back towards the town – at all the jumbled red rooftops. Whitby is in a ravine, with houses going up each side, the sea flowing down the middle, coming in through two stone harbour walls shaped like the ends of a pair of pincers. The place was teeming on land and sea: complicated, colourful little boats of all shapes and sizes were coming and going, and people were moving through the town slowly and steadily like blood in a body. Some of them (men with beer cans) were burning driftwood on the bit of beach at the bottom of our side of the ravine, and the day was so bright you could hardly see the flames.

I was looking at this fire when Bowler turned around and broke my nose with his head.

When I was down, he kicked my face. I put my hand up, and I could hear Bill pummelling Bowler and sounds like 'oof' and 'doof'. The two of them got up off the ground at the same time because some tourists were watching. My face was all moved over to one side.

'This fucker thought he'd got it sussed,' Bowler was saying. 'Get with Dean, rip the two of us off – and Neville's involved, I fucking know it.'

'No, Walt,' said Bill, looking at Bowler but pointing at me. 'He thought it was you.'

So I'd been wrong about Walter Bowler. I was trying to stop the blood with my sleeve, but after a while I gave up and turned away from the line of tourists who were walking down the gravel track through the middle of the graveyard; I sank down, tipped my head back and went cross-eyed, trying to look at my nose, pointing it in the direction of a ship on the horizon that looked like a stack of boxes moving across the sea, with a crane on the front end and a crane on the back. I didn't want to touch my nose because I was worried about what I might find.

'All right?' said Bill.

As he looked down at me, walking around in a circle, I tried to work out the state of my nose from the expression on his face. He didn't seem too worried, but then it wasn't his face.

Stretched out on top of a grave in that graveyard, I thought: I might as well move in here permanently because this could be the last but one day of my life, and the way Bowler was going it could be the *last*. It was the twenty-seventh of August – nothing special about that date, but there'd been nothing special about the twentieth of July 1994 when Lacey had gone under the train.

A smell of oil and beefburgers was coming up from Whitby as I looked back across the beach, at the blokes with their fire, with the air wobbling above it. Every time I breathed in, the air had to twist upwards by a funny route, going through a couple of sort of chicanes.

162

Walter Bowler seemed to have gone.

'Why did he do it?' I said.

'Walter?' said Bill. 'Or Dean?'

'Dean. The goods have got no value to anyone except the Yank.'

'But Dean is a half-wit,' said Bill, 'and that is the X factor.'

'Do you think Neville's involved?'

'No. Hold on, I'm going to call him.'

I half closed my eyes, looking away from the golden blur in the sky, and hearing Bill starting to make his call but gradually being drowned out by seagulls and surf.

Bill came back a minute later.

'I've explained the situation to Neville; if he hears from Dean he's going to tell him to get straight back to the house with the goods.'

'Then we can fucking equalize him,' said Bowler, who was back, smoking and not saying sorry.

'No,' said Bill, 'because he's got Neville looking out for him, and Dean is our guest, and you do not equalize your fucking guests.'

'Maybe he's going to try and get the cash off Butteridge and the Yank on his own,' said Bowler.

'Butteridge isn't going to go along with that,' I said, and every word hurt my nose.

'No,' said Bill. 'He'll only deal through you. He told us.'

I stood up and we walked down the Abbey steps, which lead to the top of that particular half of Whitby, which is known as the Old Town, and which does not look any older, or younger, than the other half. With me touching my nose every few seconds, we walked into some narrow streets filled with tourists, lads, lasses, police, buskers. The little shops were all spilling out into the street, selling things from stalls outside: sticks of rock, ships in bottles, that kind of thing;

every chimney pot had its own seagull. We walked through the door of a tiny pub with big brass pipes going around the walls and benches on all sides. The place reminded me of a station waiting room from the days of steam.

Bill ordered the beers, and I went to the gents to look in the mirror. At first I tried looking at my face without looking at my nose. My face was dead white and, from the front, the nose looked OK. I turned to the side and saw a person I did not recognize: the shape of my nose had changed – only slightly but enough to make me into someone new, someone new who looked older and not so dodgy, but who probably wouldn't be around for very long.

I walked back into the bar in a state of numbness. Around the walls were flower-shaped lights on twisted brass tubes, and black-and-white photographs of wooden boats full of men who looked like Mr Ollernshaw afloat. In the corner, somebody was talking in the strongest Yorkshire accent I've ever heard. Unlike York, Whitby was hardcore, and everyone in the town was full-on all the time.

My mobile rang.

'*Got 'em?*' said Butteridge.

I couldn't think of anything to say.

'Sort of, yeah.'

'That is not the answer I want to hear. *What the bloody 'ell's goin' off?*'

'Don't worry about it. We've got a bit split up, that's all.'

'Can you get to the house with the chairs for two?'

'You said one.'

'But there's been a change of plan.'

'This is the second change of plan. It's fucking pissing me off.'

It was a bit ironic, me bollocking Butteridge for changing the time of payment for the goods when we hadn't even got the goods. But there it was.

'We're getting the cash together,' said Butteridge.

'We?' I said. 'Is the Yank there with you?'

No answer from Butteridge.

'You know what?' I said. 'I don't believe in this Yank, and I don't believe in this money.'

'Fine,' said Butteridge, 'but what's the chair situation?'

'There's been a little bit of a problem; I'll get back to you.'

Butteridge hung up. The situation was doing my head in: my nose was broken, but that didn't matter because I was under sentence of death from Neville, but that didn't matter because, if I was alive, I'd only be back inside or delivering leaflets all my life.

After I'd told Bill and Bowler what Butteridge had said they carried on talking to each other, while I just stared people out who were staring at my face. At midday, the clock in the pub clanged like hammer blows, and I started crying, not that it was obvious. It stopped after a while.

We stayed there all afternoon, and I went to sleep for some of the time. When I woke up cricket was on the TV, and there was no room for any more glasses on the table.

We all stood up, and we walked, for some reason, down to the bridge that goes across the sea at Whitby, joining the two halves, Old and New. On the other side of the bridge, the New Town side, Bowler went into an amusement arcade while Bill and myself watched some blokes throwing boxes of fish around on the quay. The fishing boats were lined up in front of me – old-fashioned-looking things, but with radars, satellite dishes and aerials sprouting all over. I could see multi-coloured oil in the water and, behind me, in one of the arcades, a bingo caller was yelling through a broken microphone, 'Tony's Den, Number Ten', feeding back and distorting.

Bowler was standing outside the amusement arcade just

next to a fat clown in a plastic bubble, and all of a sudden he
had a great big grin on his great big face.

'Come in here,' he said.

Bill and myself walked into the amusement arcade, following Bowler; the Spice Girls were blaring, and some low, deep
machine voice kept croaking 'Downtime', or something like
that, over and over again. Bowler took us towards the back,
where it was quite dark, and where Dean Martin was playing
Virtual Striker Two on his own, twiddling the levers and
shouting, 'Fucking lay it off, man . . . fucking lay it off!'

Judging by the flashing screen in front of him, Dean was
beating Dean by four goals to one. He hadn't seen us yet.
When the football game finished, he climbed off the stool,
went over to some miniature horses and jockeys jerking on
sticks down a green plastic track, and started to put some
money into the machine. Bowler walked up to Dean, and
touched him on the shoulder.

Dean was cool.

'What do you fink?' he said, turning around and pointing at
the machine. 'Ver red horse?'

'It's just guesswork,' said Bowler.

'Yeah,' said Dean, 'but I fink ver red horse.'

He pressed the button for the red horse, and it won.

'Aw, nice one!' said Dean, and fifty pence fell out of the
machine.

'Now you've made one thousand pounds and fifty pence
from your stay in the north, Dean lad,' said Bill. 'You're
doing well.'

''Ere,' said Dean, pocketing his winnings and pointing at
me. 'What's wrong wiv his face?'

'I'm going to show you exactly what happened,' said
Bowler, moving over to Dean in that noisy corner, with the
Spice Girls blasting out their nonsense tune and every

166

machine clanging and banging away.

'Actually,' said Dean, backing away from Bowler, going towards Virtual Striker Two again, 'I'm fucking glad I've met up wiv you guys.'

Bowler smashed his head into Dean's face; there was a snap, and blood was connecting Dean's nose and his mouth.

'Fuckin' Walter!' said Bill.

'What did you say?' said Bowler to Dean.

'I said I'm fucking glad to see you lads,' said Dean, and Bowler nutted him again; his nose was basically on its side now, and it looked far worse than mine.

'Come on,' said Bill over Bowler's shoulder to Dean. 'We're going for a walk.'

We walked back over the little bridge, with Bowler holding Dean's arm. Dean had a carrier bag in his hands, like somebody going into court, and the whole bottom half of his face was blood, so he looked like a three-year-old who'd eaten a jam sandwich not very well.

While we'd been in the amusement arcade, a boat that looked like a railway platform made of rust had sailed right into the middle of the harbour. On the side of it was a crane with a metal grab that kept plunging down into the sea, picking up water as best it could (but the sea would come gushing out as soon as the grab was lifted), and then swinging across the deck of the boat, so the boat was cleaning itself like some massive wild animal. The crane was making the boat rock about like mad, and it looked as if everybody in Whitby was standing on the harbourside watching this monstrous sight.

Dean kept sniffing but, like me, he couldn't really do it. We must have looked like the broken nose club on an outing.

Twenty-two

We walked on to Tate Hill beach, which is at the bottom of the Old Town. It's the only bit of beach that Whitby has, and that's why it's not popular as a tourist destination with most Yorkies. Above this beach, the backs of the Old Town buildings overhang like cuckoo clocks – sticking out from a cliff growing out of a wall made of massive black stones.

This beach was where the fire had been, and the pile of wood was crumbly and ghostly; there were patches of black in the brown sand. A thick riveted pipe ran down one side of the beach, which was basically semi-industrial, dipping into the estuary like an anaconda taking a drink. But there was one old-world touch on the sands: two big wooden rowing boats coloured green, black and white, filled with oars, fishing nets, old cans of Tango and a lot of other clutter, and tied to the black stone wall underneath the biggest and lowest of the overhanging buildings: a pub.

Dean sat on the edge of this boat, shaking and skinning up, still being cool, with blood on his face like a hard red beard. His nose was just a memory, and I could see something bright and white in all the splatter – bone. Bill was standing in front of him, with his hands in his jacket pockets, shaking his head.

Bowler, a few feet away, was walking along the edge of the sea with his darts player's shirt fluttering. I was sitting on the sand near the boat, watching Bill and Dean.

Out at sea, just to the right of Bill's head, I could see the container ship with the two cranes and the stack of boxes. It had moved about two inches since I last looked at it.

'Where are the chairs?' said Bill to Dean.

'No problem,' said Dean. 'In ver car, in ver car park' – and he pointed up to the Abbey. 'Here's ver janglers, mate,' he said, throwing the keys back to me. 'Might've put a couple of scratches on it. Noffing serious, vough.'

'What were you going to do with the goods?' said Bill, talking very slowly, as if he was addressing an idiot, which he actually *was*.

'Nah,' said Dean, shaking his head, 'it's noffing like vat. I just fancied a spin in ver motor, wasn't trying to do noffing dirty or noffing.'

We were the only people on that beach; the day was turning grey, and a frisky wind was getting up – the sort of wind that tells you a storm's on the way. Bowler was walking towards Dean, with the sea coming in behind him, the little waves tickling up to the back of his feet as if they were trying to pull him back, but not trying very hard.

Bowler walked right up to Dean, and Bill's mobile went. He turned away to answer, and Dean moved in on Bowler, and Bowler moved in on Dean. They were together for about twenty seconds with Dean's spliff burning on the beach, and it looked as if they were kissing.

I went towards them, trying to grab Bowler, and his body was incredibly soft under that shirt – it was the first time I'd touched him. Dean's face was making the shape of a scream, and I could see Bowler's thumbs pressing way under the jaw. They looked like big toes, and I thought: they should not be that far in.

Bill was saying, 'Nev, get back to you', and then he started pulling on Bowler too, but Dean was falling into the boat with a big knife in his hand, and Bowler was turning back to face us. He was smiling at me for the first and only time and, as I looked down, I saw that his stomach was smiling too. His shirt was open – not ripped, just all the buttons gone, and I could see a mouth with white and pink things inside like little soft teeth and gums. Bowler fell forwards and a second later a big amount of blood and other stuff whooshed out of him on to the beach.

Bill picked him up immediately, putting him into the boat on top of Dean. Then he leapt in himself, kneeling next to Walter and Dean.

I was looking over the edge of the boat, at Dean. He breathed one breath. It was going out, and a while later he breathed another one – going in. Then – after about five fucking minutes – he breathed out again, but this one seemed to pull back at the last moment with a kind of small backwards burp. His mouth was open, he was moving his tongue, and it took me a while to work out that he was talking, but so incredibly quietly that I couldn't hear him above the waves and the wind. I put my ear to his mouth, but the sound of the clicking of his tongue was louder than the actual words coming out, so he wasn't easy to hear.

'West Ham . . . ver squad. I want to hear ver names of ver lads.'

I looked at Bill, but Dean was looking at me.

'Dean, mate,' I said. 'I don't follow football. I'm not fucking interested, you know?'

'Just ver names . . . any order.'

He hadn't bloody well heard me.

'Ian Wright,' I said. 'He plays for West Ham, doesn't he?'

'Ian Wright,' whispered Dean. 'No, mate, not any more.'

I brushed Dean's hair back from his forehead, and he became a lot better looking, or maybe I was just giving him the benefit of the doubt because he was dead. His nostrils looked incredibly black, but I knew that was only because his face was totally white. Even his clothes looked dead, his phat pants – dead; West Ham shirt – dead; Nike Air Maxes – both completely dead; his G-Shock was the only thing still going, and that surprised me: a watch ought to stop when its owner dies, show a bit of fucking respect, but then I thought . . . no, why would anything stop just because Dean Martin has died. The box-stack boat was still inching its way across the horizon, and the weather was still following the weird plan it had made earlier.

Now Bill had Bowler's head propped against the other end of the boat – the back end, the end that was nearest to the sea. Bill's face was against Bowler's, and his hand was on Bowler's cheek, just resting there, jittery, trying to sort of chivvy him along.

'Walter's gone,' said Bill after a while.

'OK,' I said, which was a weird thing to say.

There was a blue net in the boat with a tag on it saying 'Yorkshire Fisheries A67', which was tangled up with a string of cork floats as big as tennis balls; a lot of plastic bottles with handles which were strung together as well – everything in that boat was tied to everything else.

I looked down at my hands. Blood was on them, like thin red gloves.

I looked up and saw Bowler, whose polo shirt had an extra blob of red alongside the little polo player, so the shirt looked unique, a collector's item. His face was deflating, and it was starting to match the colour of the shirt – purple.

'It's a salmon,' said Bill, pointing at half a dead fish that was tangled up in the net. 'This is a salmon fishing boat.'

I didn't see the relevance of that, as I walked towards the sea and washed my hands in the little waves coming on to the sand.

'What are we going to do, Bill?' I said when I'd finished.

(My hands were still sticky, but in a different way.)

'It doesn't fucking matter – because we're both fucked anyway.'

'How do you mean, Bill?'

Bill was putting the net and the other clutter in the boat on top of Dean and Bowler, with the dead salmon as the finishing touch.

'Neville,' said Bill. 'Dean's cousin.'

I noticed black spots all around me on the beach, and thought they were coming up from the ground until I realized that it was actually raining . . . and that I wasn't getting wet. I looked up, expecting to see half of Whitby rising above me, forgetting that we were underneath the black jutting-out bottom of the pub. There were no walls around us, but there was a roof over our heads.

'This boat's quite nicely tucked away,' I said.

Bill nodded; the wind was strong now.

'Don't you think we should get away from here?' I said.

And we did.

Twenty-three

We walked off the beach with sand flying around the town, and the boats in the harbour rocking. The sea wasn't exactly rough but it was slapping hard against the harbour walls. Everywhere people were running to get away from the rain, and it hadn't even started yet. We crossed the bridge, and walked into a little pub on the New Town side that was as dark as a cave; there were no people there except a lad behind the bar wearing a baseball hat. The walls were white and lumpy, and the main thing in the pub was a massive jukebox, with different coloured moving lights pumping through tubes around the outside of it.

I bought the drinks, took off the bobble hat, and sat down at a little table opposite Bill. Neither of us was saying anything, and we both started brushing ash off the tabletop with our beer mats until we both *clicked* that we were both doing it, and both stopped. After a while, I couldn't stand the silence any more, so I stood up and went off to the bogs, which smelt of the sea.

I washed my hands, went back into the pub and sat opposite Bill again. I knew that the storm was going on outside but I didn't know *how* I knew: something to do with the brightness of the lights in the pub probably, and the tension.

'What are we going to do Bill?' I said.

'Will you stop fucking saying that?' said Bill.

I could see the signs of age on Bill: he'd move his face, and the skin under his chin would go in the same direction, but a fraction of a second later.

I went to the bar to buy two more pints and when I sat

back down, I could hear Bowler's voice in my head, bad-mouthing me: I had got them into this; I was a nonce, a death magnet.

Bill suddenly stood up, and I thought: no wonder he doesn't want to be near me.

'Wait here,' he said.

I waited, feeling the darkness building up all around the pub.

Bill came back after ten minutes, drenched, holding a bottle of White Horse whisky and a little newspaper – the *Whitby Gazette* – which he immediately started reading, so I thought: Christ, the cozzers are on to us already.

'What is it?' I said.

'The tides,' said Bill.

I was excited because I knew what was coming: action, which is what both of us needed. Watching him read, I thought: don't just sit there looking like a wuss, say something.

'That gives you the ebb and flow, right?' I said, pointing at the paper.

Bill gave me the evil eye for a second.

'In and out,' he said.

He looked at his watch.

'High water was an hour ago, so the timing's good. We're going to row Walter out to sea – and that other fucker.'

That other fucker, Dean, getting rained on – a guy who probably never knew who he was named after, a guy with no chance of ever taking over from the olden-day Hollywood wino to become *the* Dean Martin.

'What if they're not still there?' I said.

'If they're not still there the manhunt's already started, so they'd fucking well better be there.'

I put my bobble hat back on.

As we walked out of that boozer, I knew exactly what to expect because two old blokes were coming in through the door, and one was saying to the other, 'It's a blue sky up there now, it's just bloody ridiculous.'

So there'd been a strange turnaround but it wouldn't last because it was eight forty-five and the evening was closing in. The streets were filling up again, people carrying pints out of the doors of pubs, tourists running about with jumpers on their shoulders, all excited, in their nonsensical tourist way, about the changeable weather. We ran down the little alley back to Tate Hill beach, where a little old man was walking his dog. He was on the opposite side of the beach to the rowing boat but his dog was sniffing about inside the boat. Bill raced across the beach, and kicked that dog away.

It ran back to its owner, wagging its tail and trying to pretend nothing bad had happened, while Bill started trying to untie the boat from the rusty ring on the black wall, and I lifted up the net and looked at Bowler: bright blue now in the face, like some piece of old cheese. It was incredible to think that he hadn't been giving that dog grief.

Bill had unhooked the boat from the wall ring, and we both started dragging it across the sand. The dog owner wasn't watching us; the *dog* was but that didn't matter so much. As we got to the edge of the water I climbed in, but the boat wasn't yet floating; Bill was still dragging it.

'Get out of there,' he said – Bill was up to his knees in water, so that was fair comment – and he ran back on to the beach.

'We're going to need weights, Bill,' I called out.

'What do you think I'm fucking doing?' he said.

He was picking up stones from the beach. I got out to help, and when the water splashed up to my crotch I stopped breathing it was that cold. We threw stones into the rowing boat until it was threatening to sink, then we both jumped in and Bill took the oars. At first he kept missing his stroke and swearing, and I fancied having a go myself.

But soon he got into it, and we started moving quite fast towards the harbour exit. It wouldn't have looked anything from the beach, but the sea was choppy. Bill was in the middle of the boat, and I was at the front – the prow – and we were both going up and down like two people on a fucking see-saw.

On both sides of us were the two harbour walls that, from this angle, were frightening – covered in shiny green smears like bits of sea monster that had scraped against the stones, and massive rusted rings that looked like manacles for giants, with brown dribbles of rust coming down off them. At the end of each wall was a kind of lit-up barrel on sticks: green on one wall, red on the other, marking out the exit to open sea.

I thought we were making for these barrels but no . . . coming off the beach, Bill was turning hard right, and heading towards the wall on the beach side, making for a gap in it. The sea was leaping about in that gap, and I could see, coming and going in the dirty waves, wooden spikes. Christ, they're *stakes*, I thought.

'We can't go through there,' I shouted to Bill. 'We'll be fucking impaled.'

Bill stopped rowing for a second. The *boat* was leaping now, and Bowler slid across the bottom of it towards me, butting me on the foot with his massive head, totally freaking me out; but then he slid away again, and I jammed some of the net in between his head and my feet. Dean was half underneath him. Bill was glugging White Horse as the boat bobbed; when he'd finished, he screwed the top back on and threw it over to me.

'We can't go that way,' said Bill, pointing to the harbour exit between the barrels on sticks, and reaching for the oars again. There's a fucking camera there – photographs everything that comes in and out.'

How the *hell* did Bill know that?

I couldn't believe it. He'd been coming to Whitby with his wife and kids, buying ice-cream, acting the family man, and all the time he'd been thinking about how you could make a getaway out to the open sea. I couldn't blame him though, because in his position I'd probably have been thinking along similar lines myself.

I was basically in love with Bill, and the buzz of being in that boat . . . I've never felt anything like it. I just wanted to keep going out to sea for ever, rowing away from Neville and Lacey and everything.

We were feet away from the spars or whatever – bone-coloured wood flashing in the waves under the strange, smeary skies. The boat smashed straight into the first one and, for a moment, we were stuck on it; after a few seconds, though, we slowly scraped away but we were straight into a little whirlpool forming between two of the spikes, which spun the boat right round, smashing the opposite end, my end, into another of the poles, so now the boat was broken.

'We're holed, Bill,' I screamed out, like a wuss.

But the damage was high up, above the water line, and after that we were fine; we were through those fucking gravestones and I had a long drink of whisky to celebrate, although it was Bill who deserved it. He was still going, pulling out into the open sea, not glancing back at the death trap we'd just defeated. He was right on top of his game; Bill was in awesome form.

The sea kept rolling hump-backed bridges underneath us. It was definitely calling the shots but it was nothing we couldn't handle. By now we'd moved around the corner from Whitby, and the shoreline we could see was just cliffs. Rain was coming down but it was warm, casual rain, fizzing into the sea all around us, and the two of us were totally soaked in any case. Bill pulled the oars into the boat, and started dragging at Bowler, trying to get him sitting upright, and I joined in as best I could, but something about Bowler's face – a disgusted sort of look – made me think he was going to throw up at any moment, and that was too much for me; I rolled to the side of the boat, and the stuff just exploded out of my mouth.

Bill carried on working, ramming the stones into Bowler's jogging bottom pockets. Those trousers are pretty fucking shapeless and it was amazing how many stones they could take. Bill just kept shoving them in, and then came the obscene part because, while I held Bowler, Bill yanked his jogging shorts and his underpants, which turned out to be Jockeys, away from his belly, and I saw Bowler's dick, which was incredibly soft and small and white and peaceful, with not many hairs around it. Bill started piling the rocks into the underpants, like a clown putting one custard pie after another down the trousers of another clown. As he did this Bowler's head bobbed backwards and forwards, as if he was saying, 'Yes, please, keep those rocks coming.' I put a couple down there myself, to show I wasn't bottling out of the situation.

Suddenly Bill let Bowler drop back into the boat, and he started trying to get Dean sitting upright. Dean was stiffer than Bowler – his head didn't flop, and his mouth was wide open. Bill rammed a stone right in there, demolishing Dean's teeth. I was shoving smaller stones into Dean's socks before moving up to the pants, where Dean's todger was coiled up, circumcised and a horrible colour, the colour of fucking West Ham. I started to feel sick again, but I carried on loading.

Bill had stopped, though.

'What's up, Bill?' I said, but I knew the problem: Dean's

clothes were tight-fitting, and it was hard to fill them with stones. Bill was taking slugs of White Horse; he threw the bottle over to me again.

'We're running out of stones,' he said. 'Walter's probably going to sink . . .'

He dragged his soaking sleeve across his eyes.

'Don't know about the other fucker, though.'

'Why don't we tie Dean to Bowler?' I said, even though I couldn't see any bits of rope.

'What kind of fucking idea is that? If Dean's going to float, he's going to pull Walter up, isn't he?'

'Yeah,' I said, 'but if Bowler's going to sink, he's going to pull Dean *down*, isn't he?'

Bill was looking pissed off; he didn't really like it whenever I showed initiative, or maybe it had just been a crap idea.

We loaded some more stones on to Dean as best we could and, seeing as he was sitting upright and ready, shoved him over first.

I just said, 'Sorry, Dean, mate', as he hit the water, and Bill gave me the eye.

Bowler made a bigger splash, obviously, doing a backward somersault and tipping over to one side slightly before disappearing.

Bill was already rowing back to the shore, which was just two lines of different shades of blackness by now. I hadn't expected him to say anything when Bowler went over, but I did think there might've been a short *delay* because Walter Bowler was Bill's best mate after all.

The sea had calmed down by now, and I could hear everything: the spare water trickling along the oars and falling into the boat as Bill rowed; the creaking of the boat; the oars rattling in their metal holders. Now that there was nothing to do, my mind was running riot again: there ought to've been a fucking vicar, there ought to've been a priest, there ought to've been an undertaker – even Lacey had had those things. We were way out of order.

At that moment my mobile started ringing.

'Butteridge,' I said.

'Leave it,' said Bill, rowing.

We went back through those bastard stakes and I didn't notice and I didn't care. I wanted to lean over the edge of the boat and go into the sea, and say sorry to Cameron Lacey because it was horrible being dead. You had no fucking dignity, and as soon as it happened your whole life looked ridiculous because there was no chance of changing all the nonsense: Lacey with his railway timetables and Sea Cadet uniform; Dean Martin and his Tommy Hilfiger gear; Bowler and his ultimate dream of no longer having to nick bikes for a living.

Bill rowed us right on to the little beach – nobody was there – and then just flopped forwards on his rowing seat. After a while he looked up at me.

'No wonder salmon fishing is dying out in this fucking country,' he said.

We slopped back up the Abbey steps, dripping water, knocking back whisky. I thought: this is good, because it looks like we're two drunks who've just been having a laugh, but since when have two drunks been totally silent? We were more like two ghosts than two drunks.

Twenty-four

Volvo 240s are nonsense vehicles but at least they've got smiling faces. Mine was snarling now, though. Dean had just about abolished the front end.

'The chairs are still OK,' I said to Bill, and it was true – they were still in the back, covered up with the blanket, but Bill was saying nothing, just standing there in a big dark car-park puddle with an empty whisky bottle in his hand. He turned around and started walking back towards the steps.

'Where are you going, Bill?'

I followed him, through the floodlight beams of the graveyard, feeling like a death magnet; all around me people die, but I keep going. Bill's silence was freaking me out. He was about twenty yards ahead of me, and I shouted out to him: 'I don't think there *is* going to be any money, Bill. I *did* think there would be, but now I've sort of lost faith you might say.'

My voice echoed across Whitby, and I put my hand to my face as I started moving again. Basically, one side was bigger than the other. It was like exploring a new planet.

We were back in the town now, stepping over little gurgling streams of water running down the alleyways. In the pubs there were just the odd few people chatting to barmen, but there was no action because last orders had been called.

Bill walked on to the Esk Bridge, boats rising and falling on the rolling water to either side of him. The railway platform was tied up there, all quiet now with its sea grabber stashed away.

I followed him over the bridge, being hit constantly by

blasts of wind racing in from the sea. I stopped for a minute, and pressed one nostril down with my fingers, and fired some blood and snot on to the ground. Ahead of me, Bill had also stopped. He was looking into a lit-up window at a lace curtain, a lamp made out of an old bent bottle, and a faded, cardboard sign saying VACANCIES.

Bill turned the corner of the building and knocked on the door. A big, hard-looking guy opened up, and you could see straightaway that he should have been down a mine instead of doing this job.

'I need a room for the night,' said Bill.

It freaked me out, that 'I'.

'There are two of you, though,' said the man.

'I need a room as well,' I said, and just then the wind blasted the hair on all our heads to the left.

'I've got one double,' said the man, when the wind had finished its little stunt.

'That's fine,' said Bill.

'You're going to sleep in the same bed then?'

'We'll work something out.'

So Bill wasn't ignoring me; he was going to *sleep* with me. The man let us in, and we walked up a dark staircase that smelt of old breakfasts. The bed-and-breakfast man, with his rattling janglers, was more like a screw than any sort of host, and the only thing he said going up the stairs was: 'I want you out by ten o'clock.'

I thought . . . fucking charming.

When we got to the top room in the place though, all hell broke loose. Opening the door with a crash, the guest-house screw shouted, 'Electrics!' and started turning the lights off and on, thumping the switches with his fist.

'When's breakfast?' said Bill, lying down on the bed while all this was going on.

The bloke stopped thumping the lights.

'Eight o'clock.'

'Eight o'clock till when?' said Bill.

'Eight o'clock till eight o'clock,' said the bed-and-breakfast man, and he walked out.

'Thinks we're a pair of queers,' said Bill.

He was sitting up, taking his shirt off. His body was actually quite white, and the hairs on his chest were grey. He was older than me.

He stripped down to his boxers, walked into the bathroom and started trying to slash, but it took ages before anything came. I couldn't stand the wait, so I pulled back a gritty net curtain, looking out through the rattling window at the black sea banging about. I was on the spot and my time was nearly up; this could be my last night but all I was thinking about was . . . it's embarrassing, sharing a room with Bill.

Turning around towards Bill, I said, 'Napoleon was a very slow pisser as well.'

So was Wilkinson but I didn't mention that.

Bill said nothing, but then the trickle started. When it had finished – and it didn't last long considering the amount of whisky he'd put away – he started cleaning his teeth with water and his finger, which made me feel like a slob because I hadn't even thought of doing that. Then he was back on the bed with his mobile; I could hear the little bleeps as I looked out at the sea going mad.

Bill was talking to his beautiful wife, and I tried not to listen. It sounded lovey-dovey at first but I slowly figured out that he was swearing all the time.

'How *is* the wife?' I said to Bill when he'd finished.

'She's a fucking addict,' he said.

He sat down, fiddling with the phone a bit more.

'Neville's called twice,' he said.

'What's he after?'

Bill sat still for a moment, chewing on nothing.

'What's he after? He's after Dean. Dean is his cousin. He looks out for him.'

He took the semi-automatic out of his jacket pocket, and dropped it on to the bed. He lit a cigarette, and sat there smoking with his shirt off.

'We'll need money,' I said.

'You're getting it now. So you get on to your friend Mr Butteridge, you tell him to meet us at the Old Railway Bridge at twelve o'clock tomorrow.'

I called Butteridge while Bill ripped some skin off one of his toes and just kind of dropped it on the floor. There was no answer from Butteridge so I left a message. Sitting up in bed, Bill watched me do it, and when I put the phone down, he nodded. Then, without asking me, Bill got into bed and turned out the light.

Twenty-five

Standing in the dark, I thought, Neville's got two reasons to kill me now. But he could only do it once – that was the good news.

I put on the bobble hat, picked up my DJ bag, walked out of the room, and down the breakfast-smelling stairs. I started walking fast through Whitby. The sea and the sky were calming down a bit now, both turning a nice, peaceful blue-grey colour, with just occasional blasts of wind; the sea was slopping against the sea walls, and the pretty boats were bobbling in quite a relaxed way.

Walking up the Abbey steps, I took out the mobile and called the second Cooper; Cooper, the brother of Cooper. He was there – he was always there – sounding a bit high. In the background I could hear cars: not real cars, but cars in a film.

'Yeah,' he said.

'You know who I am?'

'It's midnight, Mr Twenty Grand.'

'Well, so what?' I said, taking the Abbey steps two at a time, going past the graveyard like a fast shadow, and past the church at the top of the steps which is like a church made out of seashells, with a lot of extensions.

'You sound confident,' said Cooper, 'so we'll see you tomorrow.'

'I might be a bit late, though.'

'Well, tomorrow ends at midnight, so any time before then. Neville's going to be here. You can meet him in person.'

I clicked 'off'.

He was a real bugger, that Cooper: every time I called him I expected him to say, 'Actually, we were just all having a laugh', but he never would.

There are two car parks at the top of the Abbey steps: long stay and short stay. Dean had put the broken Volvo in the short stay; it was still there, and so were the chairs, but there were also two other Volvo 240 estates close by, which was kind of intriguing. The first one, X reg., had a *London A to Z* on the back seat. It was a good omen, and I just knew I'd be able to get into that motor . . .

But I couldn't, so I moved on to the other Volvo, a Y reg with a massive inflated dinosaur, and sand all over the back seat. I got into this with the second key; pulled away feeling my new nose and listening to the sound of jumbled church bells floating up from the town. It was midnight, Count Dracula time. In the story, he came to Whitby in the shape of a dog. Don't ask me to go into details.

The 240 was a stick shift but very smooth, smelt of suntan oil – a good-time car, what with that dinosaur on the back seat. There was plenty of petrol in the tank, and at twelve fifty I was walking up to the front of the Butteridge house, which is round, like the back of a boat – the stern – remembering the first time I'd been there, remembering Dean, also Bowler, Lacey and Christine. So many people were dying . . . it just seemed like the in thing to do. The words to 'Don't Fear the Reaper' came into my head: 'Forty thousand men and women every day . . .' Like a bloody advert for death.

I rang the bell and knocked the knocker. I could hear Butteridge inside, shuffling up to the door.

'Buggeration!' he said, opening up. 'What the fuck is it *now*?'

He was looking over my head, didn't seem to've clicked to the fact that it was me at all; and he was shit-faced as usual.

He looked down at me from his doorstep.

'You need a doctor.'

Well . . . it's not what you want to hear.

Butteridge was wearing a long red dressing-gown, and his hair was all over the place, not even pretending to cover the top of his head. At the bottom of his throat was a pink V. Underneath that . . . it didn't bear thinking about.

I followed him into the kitchen.

The first time I'd met Butteridge, he'd been on whisky miniatures, but there was nothing miniature about the bottle of whisky standing on the kitchen table now. Next to it was a glass and some sort of letter. There was also the little beatbox, playing tinkly folk music. Butteridge walked over to the sink and pulled out a bottle of Dettol from the cupboard underneath. He ran water into the sink, poured in some Dettol, and instantly made a smell like YOI.

'Have you rounded up the bloody chairs yet?' he said, turning the tap off.

'Yes,' I said.

'Ahm reet glad ter 'ear it.'

'That's for you,' he said, pointing at the sink.

'Have you got the dough?' I said. 'Because if not, get out of England. Bill's desperate for cash, and he's not going to handle it in a reasonable way when you don't pay him.'

'Wash your face,' said Butteridge.

It was like being ten years old, and having a dad.

'It's a rum do . . .' said Butteridge, as I took the bobble hat off, and started washing, sliding my soapy fingers over all the lumps and bumps, thinking: at least they aren't brambles, there's nothing worse than brambles.

'*What's* a fucking rum do?' I said, drying my face on a Butteridge tea towel that had a picture of some ruined monastery on it.

'*Ah can't seem ter pin t'Yankee bloke down to owt definite.*'

'But – for Christ's sake – does the bloody Yank even *exist*?' I said.

Butteridge was rolling his head slightly, in time to the little olden-day dancing tune on the beatbox, which sounded like 'Greensleeves', but wasn't.

'He exists all right, and you'll get your money. It's just sorting out the details that's the bugger. Wait here. I'm getting dressed.'

He went out of the kitchen, and I read the piece of paper with my face glowing and stinging more and more every second: 'We regret to say that your submission to the *Danby Observer* is unsuitable for publication.' This was in print; underneath, somebody had scrawled, 'Please make all future submissions by e-mail.'

I was putting the piece of paper back down as Butteridge walked into the room.

'I like that word, "submission",' he said, watching me.

He was fully dressed in some crazy casual outfit – caravanning gear.

'I'm just off for a walk,' he said, and he just bolted out of the front door. Grabbing the bobble, I followed him. '*Put t'wood in t'oil,*' he shouted back at me from halfway down his cobbled road, and I slammed the door behind me.

We skirted fast around the Minster, and, as we walked, I looked up at the tower, keeping my eye on the top as I moved, playing a game I'd played with Lacey. The tower would look as though it was going to fall down on top of you, punish you for whatever you needed punishing for. I couldn't get it to do the trick again, though; the Minster had lost interest in me.

'Where are we off to?' I said to Butteridge, as we turned into Museum Street – dark trees, dark road, Bar walls, like

188

ghosts of walls, to the right of us. We passed a shop that sold jumpers, and a little café where you could get a nice cup of tea and pretend you were living in the bloody past, then the little shops that sell fudge, and pot cottages and teddy bears, and T-shirts with pictures of the Minster on them, and teddy bears wearing T-shirts with pictures of the fucking Minster on them.

'Most nights,' said Butteridge, 'I go to the station for a bag of crisps.'

'Why?' I said.

As he walked (and he was going bloody fast) Butteridge shrugged – I could tell from his back that's what he was doing.

'I like crisps,' he said, looking straight ahead.

'But why do you get them at the station?'

'Vending machine,' said Butteridge, still not looking at me.

When we walked through the wide arch in the walls, to hit the station approach, Butteridge seemed to come alive again as if being in the *old* city had actually been freaking him out.

'You heard of Credit House Automated Payments System?' said Butteridge suddenly. 'It's a method of transferring money internationally – cleared funds I'm talking about. That's how the Yank says you're going to get your money, but you'll get the cash instalment first.'

'I still don't know how I'm going to handle twenty grand, if I ever get it. I haven't got a bank account.'

We were outside the station now, and the pointers on the big clock hanging outside the front lurched around to half-past one. I don't like the station; it's got a bad vibration, like something electrical that's been left on too long. And there are trains in there.

But I was following Butteridge in, past the taxi rank where there was one car, and one sleepy driver wearing a cardigan inside it. The station was full of yellow light, and no trains so far. Butteridge drifted off to the vending machines, and I stood on platform 3, listening to some bleary porters flinging mail bags from one trolley to another. The first porter was shouting out the names of the places the sacks were going: 'Donny, Huddy, Ponty, Braddy . . .' The trolleys looked old, with metal wheels that looked in need of tracks.

A little electrical baggage wagon came rattling down the platform: one little mini-train pulling three little mini-carriages, driven by a tiny guy with a massive beard. At first, because of this little sub-train, I didn't hear the real one approaching, but then it was right alongside me: the noise of hammers and massive electrical fuzz, so loud that when I looked at the porters, still throwing their bags and still shouting, I couldn't hear them. The little guy on the baggage wagon was shouting now as well, and his mouth was a wide open red hole in the tangled hair of his beard, but I couldn't hear *him* either. I turned towards the train, and that was when the bacon slicer started – a scream that was drowning out the train that was drowning out the blokes, that was drowning out the whole rest of the world, and not letting me move or do anything but see what was written on the shaking dusty wagons two feet in front of my face: 'World Bulk'; 'World Bulk' over and over again. This killer still on the loose.

Butteridge was next to me, shaking a bag of crisps, talking but I couldn't hear. He put the crisps between his hands and banged the bag, which was his way of opening it – there would have been a noise there, but the guy was in a silent film as far as I was concerned.

But I heard him bite the crisp, because the train had gone. He pulled a face and started shaking the bag again. I could hear that too, and the porters, still calling: 'Wakey, Hally, Sheffy . . .'

190

Butteridge looked at me, holding his crisp bag.

'You were involved in a railway accident. I read about it in the paper.'

'It was really the other guy who was *involved*,' I said. 'I could see what was going to happen but I didn't warn him.'

Butteridge nodded, putting a crisp in his mouth.

'I was jealous of him.'

'Buggeration!' shouted Butteridge, spitting out the crisp. 'What the fuck's wrong?'

'It's a fucking rogue packet.'

'What do you mean?'

'No fucking salt.'

He put the bag in his pocket.

'These things happen,' he said.

We walked out of the station, back through the Bar Walls, back to the top of Museum Street: the Minster was still there. We stopped at the bottom of the Tower.

'What about your folks?' said Butteridge.

'My mother's dead, and I never knew who my father was.'

'Lucky,' said Butteridge, nodding.

'Lucky?'

'Yeah . . . about your old man anyway. It looks like I'm getting divorced.'

'Big surprise,' I felt like saying, but I held it in.

'Call me on the mobile at eleven,' said Butteridge, '. . . *an' we'll sort us sens out.*'

Twenty-six

I was back in Whitby at four o'clock. In the short-stay car park I worked fast because there was a big silver crack widening out over the sea. The day was happening. I moved the four chairs out of the Volvo that Dean had totalled into the one with the dinosaur in the back, except that I burst that with a burnt match and stuffed it into a bin.

I drove into the middle of Whitby, to the car park outside the railway station, and slept for an hour in the driver's seat. When I woke up at six fifteen the sky was bright blue and full of seagulls. I called Bill on the mobile but he was switched off. I went into the station, bought a Biro and a postcard with a picture that was totally black except for the words 'Whitby by Night' – it was a joke, except that it wasn't funny. I wrote on the postcard and put it into the back pocket of my Lee jeans.

At six forty-five I started running through steep, sunny streets back to the guest house, and I was there by seven. In the daylight it looked almost clean. I walked upstairs, and knocked on Bill's door, but there was no answer so I walked in.

It was dark but Bill sat up in bed straightaway.

'Shall I open the curtains, Bill?'

He hadn't missed me. I opened the curtains and the shabby window, and there was the sea, shining. Bill was lighting a cigarette; I turned towards him, with the sea glittering behind me like a big jewellery box.

'Big day,' he said. 'Got hold of Butteridge yet?'

'Yeah,' I said. 'We're to go to York and call him at eleven.'

'More noncing around,' said Bill, but he didn't seem that

pissed off. He started chopping out lines on the table next to the bed, and I did two while he was in the bathroom; after a while he started talking to his wife in there, and doing a crap at the same time.

He came back out putting the shooter in his jacket pocket. I was back over by the window, looking out at the sea. I leant right out and took a big deep breath that seemed to keep going into my lungs for ever – it was the effect of the charlie.

Looking at the sea, I thought: Bowler and Dean are in there. As far as Bowler was concerned, I felt nothing; the bottom of the sea was a good place for him to be, but with Dean . . . the feeling that he should still be about was strong, and I just knew it was going to keep increasing.

We walked down the smelly stairs to the dining room, a pink place with a chirpy man on the radio and quiet couples all going for the full English breakfast. Bill went out and got *The Times*; he read it all the way through breakfast, but when the tea came he poured mine out first.

We settled up with the screw, who cracked a big grin when the money was in his pocket, so maybe that was all he'd been worrying about. As we walked through town, back to the Abbey car parks, I was thinking: today the Butteridge thing has got to turn out to be real; I've got to get my hands on my cut; I've got to get that down to London, where Neville's got to agree to settle up, and then not actually equalize me. The chances of it all coming off were small, but I felt OK because of the charlie, and because I was sort of resigned.

On our way to the station, I explained to Bill that I'd swapped Volvos.

'Are you speeding?' was all he said.

He wasn't being heavy with me, just quiet. Drifting back to York on the A64, Bill's phone went and he switched it off.

'Neville,' he said.

I looked across at him a couple of times after that, and he was sitting there, shaking his head. I'd never seen him do that before. He didn't say anything until we got to Clifton Green, where the traffic was heavy.

'Race day,' said Bill, and it was.

I parked in Lord Mayor's Walk, and we swept into the middle of town under Monk Bar with its little toilet-roll turrets looking white and clean and its medieval badges and crests and whatever shining in the sunlight.

In the middle of town, the church bells were going; fiery-faced men were swaggering up and down, covered in rosettes and coloured tags like prize bulls, with their women walking behind wearing fluttering, flowery dresses and holding white handbags.

We went into Parliament Street, where there was a tiny tinkling plastic steam train – full of kids – going round and round with its front end right up against the back. A bent old *Leader* seller was yelling 'Lee-er!' next to his little barrow, and some Morris dancers were leaping around the corner from Pavement in time to a small moving band that was following them. The whole scene put me in a daze, and Bill was the same. We had so much riding on this day, and yet somebody had built Toytown all around us. It made it hard to concentrate, and it wasn't until eleven fifteen that I called Butteridge.

He sounded sad, and very far away.

'Go to the pub,' he said. 'Then call again at midday.'

'What pub?'

'Any pub you like, you've got a lot to choose from. Just kill half an hour.'

I told Bill, and he listened to me with the Morris dancers going behind him, and his right hand in his jacket pocket. I knew what that right hand was holding.

'We could go to the Roman Bath?' I said, but I might as

well have been talking to myself.

The pub was crowded, full of cockneys flashing their wads; some Americans too. The vibe was incredible, sunlight and smoke, shouting, but not pissed shouting – crisp. The ashtrays were still clean, which I like, and the empties hadn't started piling up. I was queuing at the bar, and Bill was behind me, fiddling with his mobile. Just as I was getting served he leant over and said into my ear, 'Neville's left a message.'

'Yeah?' I said, turning around.

'He can't find Dean; he knows Dean's fucked and he's held me responsible.'

'What does that mean?'

'He's putting me on the spot,' said Bill, sounding almost proud.

'But you knew that was going to happen anyway,' I said, as if that was some sort of consolation.

Bill was nodding, and, being the cool dude that he was, he gave me a little grin.

'That's true,' he said. 'The wife and kids are away already. No problem.'

I passed a pint of Smooth across to Bill.

'Where you all off to?'

'It's destination Europe,' said Bill. 'Ingrid's mother's place.'

'Well, that's two of us on the spot with Neville,' I said. 'I've been on there right from the fucking start.'

But Bill didn't somehow connect with this piece of news, or maybe he just didn't hear, what with all the happy racing men around us – or maybe it was because Butteridge called at that exact moment.

'*Ow do,*' he said. 'It's all sorted, get here at one.'

'Where?'

'My place.'

I pressed 'off'.

'He wants us at his place at one,' I said to Bill.

'Does he?' said Bill, and he smiled again.

At ten to one we picked up the Volvo, and both did two more lines off the back of *The Times*. I put the bobble on, and drove us right into Butteridge's street, nudging through tourists.

The street looked beautiful with the bent, olden-day lanterns bowing at each other, ivy fluttering on the walls, flowers blooming on all sides like hallucinations, and the Minster standing guard behind the houses on the Butteridge side. As Bill and myself climbed out of the Volvo, we were being eyeballed by a man in a sun hat. He had a massive palace of a house and yet a knackered-looking, hand-pushed blue mower, but the thing was probably just another way of showing off – it was probably an antique. As it mowed, it made a snoring sound. The sun was making a nonsense of my bobble hat: the sweat was rolling down from it, tickling my new nose.

Butteridge answered the door with a wine glass in his hand, staring at the Volvo. He was wearing blue jeans and a jumper without a shirt. Around his neck on a cord were some specs I'd never seen before – just plain clear plastic ones, the kind you can buy in post offices.

'You got those chairs under wraps – that's good.'

I was looking behind him, at the phone in the hall.

'Where's the other two?' said Butteridge to me.

'They're not here,' said Bill.

Butteridge walked back into his kitchen, which smelt more strongly of bananas every time I went into it. On the table was a bottle of wine, and there was a horrible electric clock above the sink that I'd not noticed before. It was two minutes past one.

'I thought we had a breakthrough when I called you,' said

Butteridge. 'The Yank phoned up and said we'd do the swap here, money for chairs at one, but now he's saying he wants to be a bit more careful, so he's *working summat else owt, an' he's gonna call me at ten past . . . Ah dunno . . . I can't thoil it.*'

'You can't what?' said Bill, who was leaning against the sink, smiling.

'Can't thoil it,' said Butteridge, who'd forgotten again that he was only supposed to be talking to me, 'I can't . . .'

'Come here,' said Bill.

'Eh?' said Butteridge.

'Come here,' said Bill.

Butteridge walked over to Bill, and Bill put his head to one side.

'You can't what?' he said again.

'Thoil it,' said Butteridge.

'Is that English?'

'It's Yorkshire.'

'But I'm from Yorkshire,' said Bill, 'and I don't understand.'

'It's dialect,' said Butteridge. 'It means . . .'

'I don't want to know what it means,' said Bill.

Butteridge sat down at the kitchen table again, folded his arms. It was gone ten past.

After a while, it was nearly one fifteen by the electric clock over Butteridge's sink.

Bill, leaning against the sink, took the gun out of his jacket pocket, put it down on the draining board, took his jacket off and rolled his shirtsleeves right up. I knew why he was doing that, and it freaked me out. When he'd settled down again the gun was in his hand pointing at Butteridge, who was drinking wine at the kitchen table, nodding to himself slightly, fiddling with his specs, and not letting on that he'd noticed the gun. Suddenly he put his glass down, and leant

197

back with his hands behind his head. Bill moved slightly, putting the gun more in Butteridge's direction without seeming stressed at all – Bill looked beautiful and in control. By contrast I was sweating under the bobble, still feeling broken-nosed. Nobody was talking; it was one twenty.

'Can I smoke?' said Butteridge at one twenty-five.

'No,' said Bill, which was just pointless cruelty.

At one thirty, Butteridge's wine was finished, and he moved the glass once across the table like a chess piece.

'How long have I got?' Butteridge said to Bill, and the phone started to ring. It was a very lovely noise.

Twenty-seven

'Rowntree Park gates,' said Butteridge, walking back into the kitchen after talking on the phone. 'We take the chairs there now.'

Who'd have thought that one would come out of the hat? I hadn't been to Rowntree Park since I was a tiny kid.

Bill put his jacket back on, put the gun in his pocket and we all walked out of the house and squeezed into the front of the Volvo – I was driving as usual, even though I was the youngest. Butteridge started with his mobile phone in his hand but, going down Micklegate, he put it into his jacket pocket. We drove in silence through the happy race-day crowds of central York, and parked in silence on Terry Avenue, which is between Rowntree Park and the Ouse. A multi-storey tourist cruiser was sliding past on the river, and every tourist on it was watching us.

'We've got to get out, leaving the chairs in the car,' said Butteridge. 'Then we've got to stand behind the bogs near the bowling green in the park.'

Bill said, 'Why?'

'We're being watched. If we're behind the bogs we're out of the way, and the Yank and his mates can take the chairs out of the car.'

'And what's to stop them just taking the chairs and fucking off?' said Bill.

'Well,' said Butteridge, *'yer've got me – 'ostage sort o' thing.'*

'But maybe they've already written you off,' said Bill. 'Like everybody else.'

On the other hand, though, what did we have to lose, except some nonsense-case chairs? So we climbed out of the Volvo anyway, leaving it unlocked, and walked through the park gates, being stared at by people eating ice-creams, and about a hundred kids climbing on a climbing frame that looked like a UFO. Doves were flying above our heads, coming from their house in the park – the dovecote – which looked like a windmill without sails. We walked past a man and a woman ballooning out of their little white shorts, carrying cameras and licking lollies. I knew they were Americans and, looking around the park, there were a lot of other strange-looking individuals who could have been Americans as well, but Butteridge – who knew what *the* Yank looked like – was walking with his head down, giving nothing away.

We carried on, past a bowling green surrounded by dark green monkey-puzzle trees. All the players were in white and beige, getting-ready-to-die clothes. One of them called out, 'Afternoon, Bryan', but Butteridge said nothing, and the bowler looked back at the game when someone else shouted out, 'Wicking in!' A bowling ball that was trundling along the grass slowly started changing direction.

Behind the bogs, though, everything was different: stinking bin bags, broken glass, dented lager cans, smell of piss. Someone had written 'U can suck my dick' on the wall, and we were surrounded by trees and rubbish and shadows – anything could happen to us in this spot. Butteridge took out his mobile, and Bill took out his gun, but it was Butteridge's mobile that went off first.

He took the call, and said, 'That was quick', into the phone. Then he looked up at us.

'That were t'Yankee feller. We're ter go back ter t'car.'

'Why?' said Bill again.

'Ter pick up t'loot,' said Butteridge, so no wonder he was *on*.

200

We moved out from behind the bogs, and walked back through the park, the same lot watching us as before. Yet again one of the bowlers said, 'Afternoon, Bryan', and Butteridge still didn't say anything, but there was a bloody massive grin all over his face.

Coming out of the park gates I saw that the chairs had gone from the back of the Volvo, and that the back seat was up. Getting closer I saw an old light-blue rucksack on the driver's seat and, opening the door, I saw a cloth badge sewn on to the rucksack: 'UCLA' it said, with the letters going round in a circle. The same tourist cruiser was going past as before – but this time in the opposite direction – as I put the rucksack on my knees, and took out a bundle of twenty-pound notes as thick as a brick. Bill was in the back seat, looking over my shoulder, and Butteridge was on the passenger seat, looking across the gear lever, smelling of wine and smiling.

The notes were wrapped in a green paper band with 'S.G.S.' stamped on it in red – I didn't know what that meant. I put the bundle next to the gear stick and reached back inside the bag. There were a lot more of the same in there.

Butteridge was looking straight ahead, talking quickly to himself: *'Bloody Edward Johns, ah fuckin' luv 'im, ah've fuckin' done summat that me fuckin' dad could never do, ah've fuckin' pulled it off, ah can't fuckin' believe it.'*

When I looked into the rear-view, though, Bill's face was too close.

'What?' I said, but the gun was in the back of my neck so I *knew* what.

'Pull away,' said Bill.

'Where to?'

'Somewhere nice and quiet.'

I started the engine, and Butteridge hit the dashboard with his fists.

201

'Buggeration!' he shouted.

'You', said Bill to Butteridge when the shout had faded away, 'pass the fucking bag back here.'

Butteridge passed the bag through the gap in the front seats as I started going at twenty miles an hour along the side of the river, with the gun sticking in my neck and probably making a bruise. When the river road stopped, and we hit Bishopthorpe Road, we had to make some sort of decision about where we were going.

'What do you want to do?' I said to Bill.

'I'm still thinking.'

While he was thinking I drove slowly back into the middle of town because there were more people there, and more people meant the gun couldn't go off quite so easily – maybe.

At Exhibition Square, Bill said, 'OK, Gillygate.'

Another one out of the hat. So we went down there.

Wagon and Horses, Bay Horse, careful Yorkies wobbling on bikes, Salvation Army place, a cake shop full of white ladies in white paper hats – all that normality on the other side of the glass, but in the car a gun hidden from pedestrians by the headrests of the front seats.

'What are you going to do, Bill?' I said again.

No answer to that.

Approaching Lord Mayor's Walk, though, Bill said, 'You *know* what I'm going to fucking do.'

'You're going to do me and Bryan.'

'Who's fucking Bryan?' said Bill, and Butteridge half turned around, as if he was going to introduce himself.

'Face front,' said Bill.

'You'll be all right if you do what I say,' said Bill to me, 'but that silly cunt's had it.'

'Why, Bill?' I said. 'It's not as if he'll go to the cozzers.'

'Can't be doing with nonsense cases,' said Bill, 'and Wal-

202

ter's dead because of him.'

That's not right, I thought: Walter's dead because of *Walter*. We were in Heworth Green now, approaching the ring road and the road to the coast.

'Stop the car,' said Bill. 'I'm letting you out.'

'Both of us?'

'Not him.'

'Off you go,' said Butteridge, looking straight ahead.

Until now there'd been people all around, and Butteridge and myself could have got out of the car and walked away but we hadn't thought of doing that, and now it was too late. There was a square-shaped old biddy drifting along the pavement about a quarter of a mile further out of town, but she wouldn't be enough to stop Bill's gun. So I just pressed my foot right down on the accelerator.

Forty miles an hour, past the biddy, Bill roaring in the back, sixty, hitting Malton Road, moped in front, fields on right-hand side, that's Heworth Stray, sunbathers, forty-mile-an-hour-limit sign, sixty miles an hour round the roundabout, round the roundabout again with every horn ablaze, man, out of the roundabout, sign (A1237 Harrogate Road), ninety miles an hour, one hundred and ten, Butteridge – hands over eyes, Bill shouting, me shouting at him, 'Drop the fucking piece then – out of the fucking window with it!' – passing every car on the road.

Another roundabout, parent-and-child sign, big caravan shaking on the back of a lorry, round the roundabout at sixty, round the roundabout again, weird, high noise, it's the tyres, draught behind me, hair blowing forward, free-feeling around my neck.

'It's gone now,' Bill was quietly and quickly saying. 'It's out the window now, all gone and been and finished.'

So I came off the roundabout, hitting the A1237 again, but

203

in the opposite direction, and slowing down.

We were back in Gillygate five minutes later, and doing twenty, when Butteridge took his face out of his hands and looked up.

'You could have been done for speeding there, you know,' he said.

I leant forward, then leant back, sort of knowing what was going to happen.

The gun was there again.

'You fucking *cheat*,' I said into the rear-view, but I couldn't see Bill's face. He was just a gun now, but there were crowds on both sides all over again, so I went from twenty to zero in one second, and the horns started going again.

'Get out!' I said to Butteridge.

We opened our doors at the same time and started walking down Gillygate with Bill following us. He had the rucksack on his shoulder, his hand on his gun, and his gun in his jacket pocket.

The two of us trotted down Micklegate, through Monk Bar, and into High Petergate with the Minster ahead of us, and the gun six feet behind. The street was packed, I saw a *Leader* seller calling 'Lee-er!', and next to him was a placard with a headline, YORKS MAN IN CASH DREAM BLOW – that could very easily have been about me. A bloke came out of the Hole in the Wall, pissed, and said, 'Look who it is', pointing Butteridge out to some mates who were still in the doorway of the pub, and couldn't be seen. The bloke was laughing.

I turned around to Bill, and said, 'Why don't you just leave us alone, you've got the fucking money', but Bill kept coming.

I wasn't looking where I was going, so I tripped over something – a little basket full of money belonging to some student who'd done a painting on the ground in front of the Minster.

'Hey!' he said, and as the coins rolled in various directions,

I saw a cozzer hanging about near by, talking to tourists. Why didn't I go up to him, and have it all out: Neville, Bowler, Dean, spill the beans . . .

For some reason I turned left next, with Butteridge following, and when we got into the garden to the side of the Minster, which is where we'd ended up, I knew we were in trouble. The place was like Heworth Green: deserted. We should have moved back into the street but I was distracted by seeing Wilkinson walking out of the gates of the Minster garden on the far side, leading a line of tourists, and pointing at the Chapter House with a stretched-out arm, like a human arrow. I knew what he was saying: 'The Chapter House dates from 1260; it is an octagonal building with a conical roof.'

I watched him go through the gates, maybe seven hundred yards off, and disappear with all his tourists. We were in the middle of the garden now, surrounded by pretty little trees, and looking at a gun. There was a silencer on it too, I noticed, even though it wasn't really needed here in the middle of this hot beautiful field in central York. I looked over to the Minster, like it was a court of appeal, but Bill pointed the gun at Butteridge, and he fired.

Twenty-eight

But it was Bill who fell over and not Butteridge. The money bag had rolled away, and he was lying on the ground with his arms spread out, and a hole under his eye that was filled with blood. I turned around, and saw somebody moving near a tree.

It was a long, thin bloke with moles on his face, a sharp beard, and long grey hair in a ponytail. He was wearing a tracksuit with wet marks that looked like piss going down one leg, and there was a semi-auto in his hand that reminded me of Bill's; he put it away in his trousers as if he was putting away his dick.

'Ow do,' he said to me, but he was mainly looking at Bryan Butteridge.

'Fuckin' Aida!' he said. *'Fuckin' Bryan Butteridge, right?'*

It was weird, because he had an over-the-top accent, so he sounded like Butteridge when he was *on*.

'Yes,' said Butteridge.

'Put it there,' said the bloke. *'Ah fuckin' love your stuff, ah'm your number one fuckin' fan. Your dad's stuff . . . that's OK, but your t'fuckin' kingpin as far as ah'm concerned.* Rambling? *Ah've not missed a single fuckin' one.'*

'Oh,' said Butteridge.

He was looking at the bloke's trousers where the gun had gone.

'Thanks very much.'

Butteridge sounded almost like a southerner all of a sudden, as if he was freaked out by meeting someone who actually liked his stuff, and could be more *on* than him.

'Are you Neville?' I said.

'*Aye. What's in t'bag?*'

'Money,' I said, kind of in shock. How did Neville end up being *Yorkshire?*

'*How much?*'

'About a hundred grand probably.'

'*Not bad fer a nonsense job,*' he said. '*Dean told me a big shot were involved, but I didn't realise 'ow big.*'

He looked at Butteridge and nodded; then he said, '*'Ow much did yer say were in t'bag?*'

'One hundred grand,' I said.

Neville seemed to think about this for a while, but he didn't exactly say anything; I think he was trying to forget about it but couldn't because the problem was: a hundred grand is not a small amount of money. He still looked as if he was thinking hard, when he walked over to Bill and kicked him in the face.

'*That's fer interruptin' mah piss,*' he said, '*. . . and fer killin' our Dean.*'

He kicked Bill again, even though he was already dead, then he carefully bent down and picked Bill up, and put him over his shoulder, spilling all the blood out of the hole in his head.

'*Where can us get rid?*' he said, looking at Butteridge.

'That's my garden,' said Butteridge, pointing to the back wall of it.

So Neville ran – with Butteridge still pointing towards the wall, and Bill bobbing about on his shoulder – to the back of Butteridge's garden. They looked just like two drunks having a laugh. Neville chucked Bill over the wall, under cover of the apple trees at the bottom of the Butteridge garden, turned around and came back to us with bloody hands, saying,

'*T'fuckin' quality of life up 'ere's just so much fuckin' better, an' that's why ah'm thinkin' o' relocatin'. After twenty year down south ah've 'ad me bloody fill. Quite a lot o' me business brings me up ere anyroad.*'

Butteridge was just too knocked back to speak, but I said, 'There's Micklethwaite . . . in Leeds.'

'*Don't talk ter me abaht that twat.*'

Twenty-nine

Half an hour later, we were sitting in the Minster Inn, which is across a cobbled square from the actual Minster, engaging in a permanent stand-off. A lot of people from the Minster – vicars and tourist guides and so on – use it as a local, but they don't go straight from the Minster to the Minster Inn. They think that would look wrong, so they take a roundabout route. It's quite funny to watch.

Today, two vicars were in, and it was interesting to see that combination of pints and dog collars. Mainly, though, the place was full of tourists as usual. There was a sleepy atmosphere, 'Wichita Lineman' playing on Radio 2, stuffed animals and antique guns everywhere, country paintings on the walls. All the windows were wide open, and every so often I'd hear, incredibly clearly, a bit of conversation from the square outside.

I was sitting in the corner, near the white fireplace with Butteridge and Neville. On the table were three pints of Tetley's, and the *New Yorkshire Leader*, which was mainly still going on about the YORKS MAN IN CASH DREAM BLOW but also had a story on the front page with the headline: MYSTERY MAN FOUND OFF WHITBY.

Basically, Dean had come back. I was sure it must be Dean, but the cozzers obviously had no idea who it was, hence . . . mystery man. He'd been bashed against rocks and, reading between the lines, there wasn't much left of his actual head. I felt sad for Dean because you only have one life and his was over. On the back of us all reading this item, I'd told Neville and Butteridge everything, but now I wasn't saying much.

Neville had put Bill in the boot of his red E-Type Jag, which he'd parked right up against Butteridge's front door. It was interesting to see such a scruffy, warty guy in charge of such a beautiful classic car, but that was the drugs business for you. The boot of the E-Type was small, though, and Bill only just fitted. I felt sorry for Bill's wife and kids. Maybe they were better off without him . . . it wasn't for me to say.

Now Neville was smoking a joint – he seemed to think it was normal to smoke joints in pubs – and reading *The Yorkshire Dales: A Coffee Table Book* which he'd taken from Butteridge's house without really asking. When Butteridge had found out, though, he'd told him he could have as many copies as he wanted.

Butteridge wasn't doing anything, just sipping his pint and saying, 'Buggeration', over and over again.

After a while I stopped thinking about Dean and, like a bastard, started thinking about the money, which was in the Butteridge basement: one hundred grand plus four envelopes, all containing the same business card. I'll say this much . . . the money launderer's name was Jay, and he worked in some part of America that I'd heard of but never thought about before.

'You saved my life,' said Butteridge out of the blue.

'Not exactly,' I said.

'You did though.'

'Maybe . . . but earlier on, you see, I killed someone.'

'Swings and roundabouts, isn't it?'

'What are you going to do with your cut?'

'Go down south, probably set up a website on the . . . you know, Internet.'

'What's the website going to be about?'

'I'll tell you that when I find out what a website *is*.'

And he lit a Hamlet cigar.

Butteridge was just putting out his match, when Neville

looked up from *The Yorkshire Dales: A Coffee Table Book.*

'*By,*' he said, '*it's a bit bloody special, this book . . . Lovely scenery.*'

'A true Yorkshireman', said Butteridge, blowing smoke, 'doesn't say "scenery".'

'*Oh aye?*' said Neville.

'He says "views": "There's a gorgeous view from this window."'

Neville just sat there for a while, taking this in.

Then he said, '*You lads on fer another?*'

As Neville pushed his way through the crowd to the bar – actually, people moved out of his way pretty fast, because he looked like a wolf – I followed him. When I caught up with him he was looking at the menu chalked on a little blackboard above the bar: minced beef dumpling, giant Yorkshire pudding with onion gravy, haddock and chips.

'You're going to kill me,' I said, and I told him my name.

Just then Neville got served, so he paid for the beers, and bought three packets of crisps, which was a good sign I thought.

'*Mrs Lacey . . .*' he said, turning around to look at me.

'You see her, do you?' I said, 'Cameron Lacey's mother?'

'*T'odd time.*'

'Give her this,' I said, and I handed over the postcard.

He looked at the front – at the blackness, and the words 'Whitby by Night'. He wasn't exactly laughing his head off. He turned it over and started reading what I'd written.

'It's confidential,' I said.

'*What yer say?*' said Neville, still reading.

'It's confidential,' I said again, when he'd finished reading the card.

'*Apology,*' he said, looking at me, holding the card in his hand.

'Yeah.'

He picked up his pint, put it down again. I wished he'd put the card in his pocket, because that would probably mean he wasn't going to do me. Instead, he was eyeballing me. You knew his eyes were blue, but it was hard to say how, because there was no real colour there.

'Ow old were this kid when yer killed 'im?'

I couldn't answer, because I would've blubbed. The pub was going on all around us, I could see Butteridge near the fireplace smoking his cigar and looking chilled out. But Neville didn't look real; he was reminding me of chair man Edward Johns – there was a sort of outline around him.

'Are you going to equalize me?' I said.

Three giant Yorkshire puddings had appeared on the bar. One vicar and two normal men came to take them away.

'I were called off by old man Lacey,' said Neville, *'last Monday.'*

'But that's when Cooper's brother called me and said it was all still on.'

'Aye,' said Neville. *'Well, they're a pair o' cunts.'*

He still hadn't stopped eyeballing me, though.

'So you were going to equalize me, and now you're not?'

'Yer seem a bit fuckin' obsessed about this,' he said.

'Sorry, Neville,' I said. 'It's just that when you've heard someone's going to kill you, you do tend to get obsessed about it – a bit anyway.'

He spoke fast: *'Old man Lacey's half mad wi' booze. His wife 'as talked to 'im, an' 'er line is . . . you've suffered enough.'*

He pulled up his tracksuit bottoms. I could see the gun swinging in there.

'Personally,' he said, sniffing, *'I don't know about that. But I'm decommissioned, yeah.'*

Neville stuffed his crisps, followed by the postcard of

'Whitby by Night', in his tracksuit trouser pockets, and set off back towards Butteridge with the beers; I followed him, carrying the rest of the crisps, feeling high.

Before we got back to Butteridge, I said, 'Sorry to bother you again, Neville, but if you're not going to kill me, that means you don't want any cash off me *not* to kill me, right?'

Neville stopped moving across the saloon bar and looked around at me, letting me see his eyes again – blue, but not blue. Over his shoulder I could see Butteridge leaning back on his stool, really getting into his cigar, even though it was only a Hamlet. Butteridge looked across at me, and I smiled at the guy as Neville answered my question: *'Don't leap ter conclusions, son,'* he said.